AF612295

PSYCHO

RUBAYATA UMEED

Woven Words Publishers OPC Pvt. Ltd.

Registered Office:

Vill: Raipur, P.O: Raipur Paschimbar,

Dist: Purba Midnapore, Pin: 721401,

West Bengal, India.

Branch Office(Operations): Hyderabad

www.wovenwordspublishers.com

Email: publish@wovenwordspublishers.com

First published by Woven Words Publishers OPC Pvt. Ltd., 2022.

ANTHOLOGY

IMPRINT: WOVEN WORDS LAUNCHPAD

ISBN 13: 978-93-91213-06-0
ISBN 10: 93-91213-06-5
MRP: Rs. 599/-

CONTENTS

FOREWORD

In a world of ever-increasing chaos where lives of people spiral in and out of control, comes a work of fiction trying to capture the essence of a social vigilante leading a double life. A reflection of our thoughts fictionalised by the author in a senstive, gripping narrative keeping your attention and eyeballs transfixed on the plot.

Rubayata is a pioneer in her own right from the unsettled state of J&K. The young author has developed and maintained a thought process independent of the political, military turbulence faced by her state. A young visionary much beyond her years who took the road less travelled for her generation. An author of two unconventionally imaginative books. The books showcased her prodigious literary talent.

I wish her all the best for her future and also I would like to see more of her work.

Best wishes,
Sapna Dhyani,
Author of Trunk Full of Sunshine

FOREWORD

Rubayata is an exceptionally talented and extraordinary writer. At such a young age, the kind of projection she has done of her thoughts is immensely commendable. I believe she has a long way to go and I am looking forward to her new book. Her zeal to be someone and establish herself as a writer, I believe would take her a long way to go. At such a young yet crucial age when mostly teenagers are either in dilemma or unclear about their vision, Rubayata knows very well where she wants to be. The best part is that she is balancing both her ambition and academics at the same time gracefully.

Not often do we hear of such talents emerging from Kashmir at such a young age, nevertheless I am confident about the fact that Rubayata is a trend-setter and she would open doors for many more ambitious people coming from a beautiful place like Kashmir. Just like the meaning of her name "Umeed" which means "hope" a lot of people including me have high hopes (Umeed) from Rubayata!

Best wishes,
Reda Shahid,
Author of An Unexpected Notification

AUTHOR NOTE

This is my first time writing a crime thriller. Although I attempted a crime sub-plot in my second novel, "Zero: Dream, Football, Alfresco," which turned out pretty great, this book revolves around the crime and justice plot. I draw my inspiration from a Japanese anime show, "Death Note," which has a gripping story revolving around the same theme. The story is set in America. It is about a person who loses his parents in an accident and is taken to an asylum. After escaping, he sets out to kill all corrupt and unjust people. His uncanny way of killing people gets him the name Psycho. As the FBI and a famous detective refer to him as 'Psycho,' events unfold to reveal his real identity. The book's primary purpose is to shed light on how justice is not always served. Many people continue to fight for the right for years and never win.

Regards,
Rubayata Umeed

I

ON THE HORIZON

It was Thursday morning, with the busy Americans leaving for work, children leaving for schools, and officers getting ready for duties. Roma just loved it, it made her feel lively. Once while writing on societies in the world, she quoted "American societies are the only ones which make me feel lively."

Roma Daniel was a college student, a journalist working for CNN network America, she was a writer too and an agent working for FBI director Mrs. Debbie Christane Rose. Yes, this girl was living four lives. She had to give time to writing books, had to rush to the site of the incident for reporting, and had to help Mrs. Debbie Rose whenever she needed it. Oh! That's a lot of work. Remember, she is a college student too, so she had to turn up with her assignments on time. But Roma loved this kind of life where you've to live four different identities. Back home she had a younger sister too, Tee Daniel, who was a high school student. Both lived in Washington D.C away from their parents. Roma was preparing breakfast and Tee entered the kitchen.

"Wow! What is it?" Tee asked.

"It's butter omelette!" replied Roma.

"Yummy!"

Both sat for the breakfast and Tee asked,

"What's the plan today?"

"Oh yeah, first I'm gonna submit a report to Mrs. Debbie and then leave for college."

"Simple plan, mine is simpler, just gonna leave for school."

So, Roma left to meet Mrs. Debbie to submit the report. Roma met her at the front door of the office, and said "Mrs. Debbie! The report. I don't have time to explain, so I'm just gonna hand it over it to you."

"I know. But thanks!" Mrs. Debbie took the report and went in while Roma left for college.

Roma studied at the Institute of World Politics. She had many friends, but they knew about her diverse identities.

As soon she reached and went to her friends, she found them whispering about something.

"What is it that you are hissing about?" she asked.

"Oh, we were just discussing the rumour hovering around the college," one of the friends replied.

"What rumour?" Roma asked.

"You see that boy there. Some in our class say he is a newcomer."

"Newcomer? Whatever. I'll catch up with you guys later in class."

Roma left for class but on way directed her way towards the boy who was standing near the staff room holding a book. None in her class dared to do something like that but she was more of a brave pal.

"My class says you're a newcomer. Is it true?" she asked.

The boy looked at her and gave her a friendly smile. The boy was slim, oddly dressed, tall, and had the most beautiful eyes. He had long hair up to the neck.

"No," he said.

"Well, then who are you?" Roma asked.

"I'm a teacher," he replied.

"You look too young for this."

"No, I don't think so. Or is it just a fancy of saying I'm fit? I am enough educated to teach in a college."

"Why did you opt to become a teacher then to continue to study?"

"Aren't you asking too many questions on our first meet?"

"Because I'm used to it for I'm a ag....... You know what I should just stop talking. See you in class."

Roma nearly revealed everything. She was, although, impressed by the boy of his uniqueness.

"Great! I didn't ask him his name. I stink!" Roma said to herself.

The boy entered the bustling class after Roma. He asked everybody's attention and begun,

"I'm HN Maaki, you're new teacher."

He opened a book and wrote on the board, 'Developed or Developing?' He asked a boy the meaning of a developed country. The boy simply answered that a country is developed if it is economically strong. HN gave his powerful smile.

"Really?" HN asked. "What is a country?"

The boy couldn't answer so he was told to sit down. After asking few more students and getting the same answer, HN said, "Isn't there anyone who can define a developed country with a good theory?"

None responded until Roma got up and asked, "What do you, sir, think is a developed country?"

"I think a developed country is one where the people's basic needs are fulfilled," HN replied.

"I don't get it," Roma said.

HN began, "Look, a country is made up of people. So, its development lies in the hand of these folk. If they are satisfied with what they have then why a country would be not considered developed. It's like if food has enough salt in it to make it tasty adding more to it would just ruin its taste."

Continuing HN said that development didn't only mean a good economic condition. Many other reasons decide whether a country is developed or not. Some countries are underdeveloped because the people there aren't satisfied with what they get. Also, no country can be considered fully developed because a point percent of its population always remains disgruntled. They usually tend to become so-called "criminals. These folks in any case affect the country's development.

"I would want you to write about it. Submit assignments tomorrow," HN said and left the class.

Roma ran after him but he entered the staff room before she could reach him.

She did get this that HN was different from any other normal person. His idea and view of even the simplest thing were deep and complicated.

A black, starry night it was. The officers for the night shift in the prison of D.C arrived.

The lights went off. Someone in the dark sneaked into the prison territory and entered one of its blocks. The criminals were just waiting, counting, and sleeping.

"I want a volunteer!"

All criminals looked at him. Hooded jacket, cap, mask, and the left side of his face hidden by his hair.

"What do you want one for?" asked one of the inmates.

"Let's just see. I want someone who's in desperate need of coming out and I assure won't be caught again," the masked man said.

"I'll volunteer! Is there something I have to do?" a criminal said.

"Jake, your name is Jake. Isn't it?"

The masked guy brought Jake out. He looked into his eyes. Jake saw red-eye and thereafter couldn't feel himself. An hour after this, the police were informed about a sudden shooting at Pod DC Hotel.

Before the police could reach there, the attacker, who was Jake, had killed himself and 49 others.

Fifteen people were injured and were taken to hospital immediately. The night just didn't go the way anyone in the hotel had planned.

Roma was with Mrs. Debbie at that time. She also went to see the situation. The hotel was in a devastating situation. The glasses were broken, chairs smashed, tables crushed and blood everywhere.

"Jeez! It's just looking like a site of war," Roma said.

Mrs. Debbie, furiously, said to the officers, "What were you doing? How could you give a criminal this much time to shed blood?"

"We are sorry ma'am. We didn't get any information of either the escape or the attack."

The following Friday morning newspaper, all of them, had the same news- "D.C rocked by overnight shooting."

ABS Times.

"Overnight shooting claims 49 lives." DC Stunned

"Deadliest shooting of the year leaves D.C in despair.

Tee held the newspaper in deep sadness.

"A sudden escape of a criminal named Jake followed by shooting at Pod DC Hotel leaves Washington D.C. and rest of America in sadness. A police report says that the information of the attack didn't reach them until only after

the officers at night petrol heard gunshots and scream on the escape of Jake.......," and she stopped.
Roma looked at her and said, "Let's see what happens." After having breakfast. Both left for their academics. On reaching the college, Roma remembered that she didn't do her assignments.
"Damn! I'm gonna kill myself."
She went to meet HN. Luckily, he was standing in the corridor.
"HN, Sir!"
"You need something?"
"A favor. I was busy last night and couldn't complete my assignments. So, could I give it to you tomorrow," Roma said.
"Well, sorry, I can't let you do that until anyone else in your class hasn't done his/her assignments."
"Ok, thank you."
Roma went to the class HN followed.
"What were you busy with, anyways? He asked
"I just have a lot of work, can't say why "Roma replied. "I'm a writer and I take care of my sister who's a high-school student. My parents live in LA, so I've to do all cooking and cleaning too."
"Who! You do have a lot of work. I live alone too but I have no siblings. I moved with my parents but both of them live in California now."
"Could we be friends outside the class?"
"Sure, I have no problem."
Roma started finding HN more interesting than she thought he would be. Then the whole class entered and they were back on the subject of whether a country is developed or not.

2

INTRODUCTION

"Jake can't escape on his own unless he had planned this because he isn't that intelligent," said Nelmon Ton, an FBI officer.

"Then it's clear he got help from outside, but who helped him?" Said, Mrs. Debbie

"Either he was part of a gang which helped him now or it's someone else," said Nelmon.

"Reports on Jake say that he worked alone," said George Haselwood, another officer, "And he had no any other relatives."

"So, the question is who helped Jake escape?" Said Nelmon.

It was clear by mid-day that the person who helped Jake escape didn't only do that but also steal a gun from the headquarters. So, either he was very intelligent or he was working for someone very intelligent. This thing kept the force thinking.

Roma sat in the library with HN. He held his head and it appeared as if he would break it.

"Aren't you getting anything?" asked Roma.

"No. I'm confused over what they've written in the assignments. They all have copied it from the internet. That's not what I wanted them to do," HN replied.

"So, you're kind of frustrated over these assignments."

"Yes. I don't have to go over something again and again. Some have even written what I said. But again, that's my idea, not theirs," HN sighed.

"They should know, even if they write the common meaning of development I'll accept it until their idea of development. I don't want them to copy

me. Phew!"

Roma looked at him and smiled.

"You're the most unusually interesting person I've ever seen."

And HN smiled back.

While Roma sat with HN, the police were in a situation of great thinking. No one was able to figure out the connection between this outsider and Jake. The outsider hadn't left a single clue of how he did all this. It was getting more and more difficult for the police as they dug deeper and deeper into the situation. Some officers said he could have been Jake's friend or cousin. But Jake had no friend and his two cousins were in jail in a remote place. With no clue of the outsider, the police briefed the report in the grief of not being able to solve the case.

In a live TV briefing the head chief, Mr. Posc, said:

"It's our misfortune that we were not able to locate the culprit or know anything about him or her. But we conclude that Jake had escaped with help of an outsider, who probably is the real culprit. Jake had not planned the shooting otherwise he wouldn't have killed himself. The outsider, who helped Jake, was the one behind this attack. The motive is still unknown. The escape took place at around 09:15 PM. The warning siren was disabled. Jake took a cab to the hotel and it was a 15-minute journey. The shooting started around 09:35 PM. Some of the victims have said that their phones stopped working during the incident. The police took some time to reach the place and Jake had done his work. We strictly condemn this attack and promise to ensure peace in near future."

The Saturday morning wasn't good in the sense that both the weather wasn't good and so wasn't the mood of the people. Nationwide mourning over the death of 49 innocent people took place and it was prayed that the injured heal soon. Though America is kind of a hub of mass shootings, this year was very peaceful until this happened.

There were protests at some places urging the government to do everything to maintain law and order. Some people, including the opposition, criticized the government for its carelessness. FBI didn't feel good either, for a case always seemed to have a clue, but this one had in it, in any way, dead ends. This case seemed as if it wouldn't get solved for years until a miracle would happen.

The whole day went in despair until another heartbreaking news rocked the whole of America. A bus carrying ten people became a victim of a bomb blast. The police reached there to find that none had survived. The two back-to-back attacks left America in a state of shock. And the FBI just started feeling that they were up against someone of very unusual brain and not normal one.

Roma sat near Mrs. Debbie.

"This is bad! Total horror," Roma said.

"I know how anyone could do this?" said Mrs. Debbie.

An urgent FBI meeting was called. They had to do something immediately. It was a 'now-or-never case. They couldn't afford to lose this battle or else the lives of innocent Americans will be lost.

"Can I say something, Mrs. Debbie?" Roma asked.

"What?" said Mrs. Debbie?

"I think this person has powers!"

"Powers, Are you crazy, Roma? Do you know what you're saying?"

"It's just an opinion."

"Crazy opinion" Mrs. Debbie got up and told Roma to leave the meeting. She left sadly.

On the way, she kept thinking of this person as having powers. When she reached, Tee greeted her with a hug and asked about her day. Roma smiled but it faded soon. She went in. Tee guessed that Roma had a day of bliss and blues.

Tee prepared the dinner, for Roma. Roma was in no mood of leaving her room. She sat in despair, holding her own written book and flipping pages, going over it again and again. Suddenly she jumped in joy and cried, "Yay! Yay!"

Tee came running in only to find her sister dancing in joy.

"Not at least anything but don't dance!" she said. "Sorry! I'm just too happy." Roma said.

"Why? You were like a lion who hadn't caught a deer, a moment ago and now you're like one having caught all the deers."

"Look, you know my recent book, don't you?"

"I even know your book which you've not published yet."

"You need to see. The first incidents written in my book are nearly as same as the two recent incidents."

"Don't tell me your book just became alive!"

Meera Saaki, Former Assistant Director of the police force in San Diego, now held the office of the director of D.C of the police force. She was sitting in her office, going through some documents when something unusual struck her. She got up in a jerk and ran to meet Mrs. Debbie.

"Mrs. Debbie! Mrs. Debbie," She called.

"What's the matter?" asked Mrs. Debbie.

"Something is interesting I need to tell you," She said, "look at this report carefully."

The report was from an international channel which said:

"A matter of coincidence or plan, but this thing will leave you thinking for hours.

While there was a shooting going on in Washington D.C, it is reported that at the very same moment the following took place:

- A truck car collision in Taiyuan, China.
- A blast near a Japanese government office in Kyoto.
- A plane crash at the India-Nepal border.
- And a blast in a car of government officials in Pakistan.

All of these incidents took place, according to world time, at the same moment. The first incident in China took 3 lives, the second one in Japan took two lives, the third one at the India-Nepal border took seven lives and the fourth one in Pakistan took four lives.

"This unusual timing of the attacks has posed a question of concern on an international level."

1. Debbie and Meera looked at each other.

UNSC (United Nations Security Council), meeting of countries over the situation:

It's impossible that the world, especially America, is going through a situation of blood and tear, just another form of war, and the UN doesn't look over it. Having peace-maker go around the world without making peace is just not what one wants? Once the news of attacks spread in different parts of the world the peace-maker, UNSC called a meeting of all its members. Countries having suffered from these attacks were told to give reports.

The reports were interesting

Taiyuan Truck/car collision report:

"The truck was being driven by a young man, Young Chin who worked as a heavy shipment delivery guy. His truck was empty during the collision. The persons traveling in the car were Mr. Tian Lee and his assistant Zuan Huang. Mr. Tian Lee worked as a local businessman known to be involved in a fraud case. The truck driver and Mr. Lee and Zuan died. Luckily the car driver survived. However, Yaung didn't know Mr. Lee. Both were strangers to each other. Therefore, the case can't be deduced. It could be accidental but according to the car driver, the truck was directly heading towards the car. So, it was intentional."

Kyoto government office blast:

"The blast took place outside the office, few were injured and two died. The bomb was found hidden in a bench on which the two dead victims sat. The motive or the culprit is not known. The victims were, Hitori Tanaka and Hibichi Kunsaaki.

India-Nepal border plane crash:

"The plane left Indira Gandhi International Airport Delhi with seven passengers and two pilots. Out of seven passengers, four were government officials from Nepal and three from India. The pilots survived. The plane reported turbulence once crossing the state of Uttar Pradesh. Nearing the border, it lost communication and crashed within minutes of this."

Pakistan government official car blast:

"A car carrying government officials from Islamabad to Rawalpindi for meeting became a victim of the blast. Everything happened all of a sudden, and we lost four government officials traveling."

After the report of the D.C. Shooting and bus blast, there was a break. Nelmon, who had accompanied the US representative in UN, called Mrs. Debbie and told her everything.

One thing, which Nelmon concluded, whoever was behind all that, was attacking the corrupt, the rich, and the criminals. But the person behind it seems to be a ghost!

3

UNUSUAL PARADOX

Mrs. Debbie grouped all the information, she knew. There were many conclusions.

Either there was a common person behind the attack or a common group. Otherwise, it was a mere coincidence and nothing else.

If there was a person behind all this, probably he had a vast network of communication with people around the world.

If it's a group, it's very large, with members from different countries.

"But what was their or his motive," thought Mrs. Debbie.

The report Nelmon gave suggested that the motive most probably was the elimination of corrupt people, rich folks, and criminals. This group or person surely was working cautiously to avoid mistakes so they or he doesn't get caught.

Nelson also arrived soon and with him brought really good news.

"Mrs. Debbie, I have got great news!" he said.

"Just say the culprit has been found," said Mrs. Debbie.

"I talked to some professional case solvers in UN and one of them has agreed to help."

"Who?"

"Famous UNSC detective John Waven."

"Really?"

"Yes."

This was enough for a moment of relief. Getting help from a professional was generally good news.

Roma ran into HN in the corridor.

"You look in an emergency!" HN said

"Yeah, no. I mean yes. Oh, I came to say you something," Roma said in nervousness.

"Why?"

"I'm sorry but I can't hand over the assignment to you until next week or so."

"Sorry, I can't give you that much time."

"But I need that much time."

"Look, I'm your friend out of the class and a teacher in the class. And as a teacher, I won't give any extensions."

"Please! I want to write on the topic but I'm busy this week!"

"No!" HN said strictly.

"Okay," Roma said, a little scared.

HN left and entered the class. After the class was over. HN went to the library. Roma came in, to see if he was okay and not angry anymore.

"Why are you so busy? The reasons you said are okay but you still get time to do work, don't you?" HN said.

"I can't tell you the reason, HN," Roma replied.

"Yeah, you can't say that to your friend, can you?"

"I am sorry I can't tell you, goodbye!" Roma left.

HN stood for a moment, thinking, and then ran after Roma.

John Waven arrived at the airport and was given a warm welcome. George Haselwood had come to pick him up. On the way to the office. George explained everything to John.

John was directly taken to Meera's office, where Mrs. Debbie and Meera were waiting with Nelmon.

"Welcome, John Waven. I'm Mrs. Debbie Christane Rose, Head Director of FBI," Mrs. Debbie introduced herself.

"I'm Meera Saaki, Director D.C. local police."

John looked at Meera and winked and then moved to Nelmon. Meera whispered to Mrs. Deeba." He looks flirty."

"I'm Nelmon Ton."

"Nice to meet you all. George explained to me everything. And it seems a very interesting case."

John was looking at reports and statements from victims. While he was doing so, an officer with a box in hand entered. He handed over it to John and said it contained some photos. These were taken by the camera in the prison block. But the photos, when John looked, showed only a side and back view of the sneaker. Also, the photos were in black and white and the color of the sneakers dress couldn't be figured out.

John stayed up late at night doing only one thing, staring at the photos.

Meera entered and asked, "Do you need something?"

"You," John replied.

"I meant something to eat or any other document."

"Makes more sense."

"You know you became a detective because you were intelligent and not a fool."

"Oh, you don't know the power of love."

"I don't want to know."

Meera left the room.

The doorbell rang and Tee opened the door. It was HN.

"Is Roma home?" He asked.

"No, She's out for some work but you can stay up in her room and wait, she'll come soon."

"Ok!"

HN went to Roma's room and sat, waiting for her. He looked around and found different photos, reports, and magazines. On the table was her book. He opened it and started reading it. Roma took time to come, so HN started moving around the room when she saw one of Roma's awards. It said:

'Best agent for FBI.'

"So, Roma is an agent in FBI," HN said to himself. Roma entered the room and was surprised to see him there. But she was more scared than stunned. She knew HN would know who she was.

"Oh, Roma, I was waiting for you," HN said.

"Why were you here?" she asked.

"Your sister said I could wait here."

"So, what were you here for?"

"I came to apologize for asking that much."

"No worries. Have a seat. You want anything to eat."

"No thanks."

Both sat face to face. They remained silent for a moment. Roma thought whether she should ask about anything related to her work while HN was thinking whether to say it to her or not that he knows who she is. At last, HN broke the silence and said everything. Roma looked at her award and said,

"Just don't tell anyone."

"I won't but if you keep that award open, someone else will know like me," HN said.

"I'll take care of that."

John, for the first time, felt frustrated. Nothing but the same information, no new clue. George came in, opening the door loudly.

"What happened?" John asked.

"A truck driving at a very high speed smashed into a mall. Fifteen are injured," George replied.

"Any deaths?"

"Yes, the truck driver died."

John reached near the incident. The injured were being shifted to hospital and the truck driver was lying down, dead. The detective went closer to the body to have a look when he saw something written. The truck driver was trying to give a message. But the words weren't crystal.

Looking more carefully, John understood the one-word 'eye'. Roma also arrived there with HN. She started reporting while HN went, John who was trying to figure out the other word.

"Red, it says- red!" HN said.

"Really? Are you sure?" John asked.

"Yes."

"How?"

"Look, the line curve can give us a 'P', the convex curve and a circle give 'E' and the last word is 'D' clearly it isn't 'PED' or 'BED'. Because PED is no word and eye BED doesn't make sense. So, it's Red."

"How much time did it take you to think?"

"Seconds."

John wanted to ask more but couldn't. He could not share the case with a stranger.

Roma later introduced HN to John. Both were very intelligent, that was clear to her. She thought if both worked together then it would be easy to catch the culprit. She asked John,

"Could HN work in the case?"

"No, he isn't professional or any officer. We can't reveal the case to him," John replied.

"Alright."

John, however, did wish HN to work. I could help some. After HN left, Roma told John her discovery.

"You have said that this person has powers because everything has happened like you had written and it's possible only when the person has powers. What powers anyways?" said John.

"Killing with his eye...." Roma was saying when John Interrupted.

"Eye, Red! Wait. This is true, I think."

Nelmon looked at John, with eyes wide open in surprise.

"You think that this person has powers, seriously!"

John looked back at him and nodded and shrugged.

"That's a 'maybe', right?" said Nelmon.

John nodded again. At last, he spoke.

"I think this person is psychic. Someone with not a normal mind."

"That's right," Nelmon said.

"I looked at the victims of the recent incidents. These all were," John was saying when Nelmon added,

"Rich, corrupt, or criminals on bail."

Exact! This psycho is killing in the name of justice."

Their talk was interrupted by an officer. He handed over a parcel to John. There was a letter attached.

The letter read:

"Here is something that might help you to solve the case."

John unwrapped the parcel and there was a drive-in with some photos. He gave the photos to Nelmon. Himself, he put the drive on his computer. There was a video in its folder. John opened it. The video was about the sneaker talking to Jake. John looked at it carefully and tried to hear every word clearly, while Nelmon stared at the photos trying to find a clue.

But after a moment, something else took over John's mind.

"Who had sent the parcel?" he thought.

4

WHO IS NEXT?

John moved around the room in deep thought and with. an unusual jittery expression on his face. He was not even bothered by the things in the parcel rather his mind was occupied with the identity of the person who had sent him the parcel.

Nelmon stared at his friend with a depth of concern. "Look, maybe we should pay attention to this material." John looked back and nodded.

"I can't! I can't believe this until I don't know who the sender is?"

The very moment Meera entered the room. She looked at both while they looked back.

"Sender? Who?" Meera asked.

"The sender of medicines!" John replied.

"Whose medicine?"

"Mine! I have high B.P. when I'm angry or am not able to solve something."

"Ok, good luck with you B.P." Meera was about to leave when John stopped her and said,

"If you could hold my hand, I'll feel comforted."

"But not me. Why don't try holding a doctor's hand," Meera replied.

"They aren't soft like yours."

"How do you know my hands are soft?" Meera looked down, John was holding her hands.

"Now you know why I know," John said.

Meera released her hand and murmured.

"B.P. quiet a heck of lie."

After she left, John was back to his nervous walk and Nelmon to his comforting talks. The whole day went thinking and twisting their brains. But nothing could be figured out.

When John and Nelmon came out, the whole office was empty except for a few workers and Meera.

John came to Meera and inquired about the tranquil condition of the office.

"I thought you had B.P. and needed rest, so the force went without you for a meeting," Meera replied.

"I've no B.P I lied! I'm too young to have hypertension!" john said furiously. Meera glared at him. John gulped.

"But, but, but. I'm not too young for not to be in love," John tried to calm Meera.

"Oh, now I know. You have a love disease. You seriously needed rest. Go in your room now," Meera said.

"No, no, no! I don't have any disease!"

The meeting of the officers, involved in the case, was underway with Mrs. Debbie. Roma was present there too. The meeting discussed the possible plans to catch the culprit. There were many suggestions but none of them appeared to work. All of a sudden there was a blackout. The lights went off and the doors got closed. The team was stuck inside the office in dark. Their phones stopped working and the oxygen level started dropping. There appeared a person on the screen in the room. Everyone looked at it except Roma.

"Guys don't look. He'll control you," She said.

Everyone got up and started walking towards Roma. She screamed and knocked at the door, crying for help. No one came. She threw chairs at anyone heading towards her. At last, she went below the table and hide.

But then she heard someone open the door. She came out of the table and found that it was HN. She went running to him.

"You okay? You look terrified," HN said.

"Thank God you came," Roma said.

She hugged him while the other members in the office fell unconscious.

In a moment, everything was cleared and Roma sat down with HN outside in the park.

"What were you doing there?" She asked.

"I came to give you something. I was waiting outside when I saw smoke coming out of your cabin. So, I came to check where I found the door locked," HN replied.

"Lucky am I!"

"Yes!"

When John was informed about the sudden attack on the meeting, he came running to the place. There the officers were being taken out unconscious. Roma sat near HN and John asked about everything.

"John, this is serious. Everything is going according to what I've written!" Roma said.

"Unusual! We need to talk," John took Roma in a corner and said,

"If this is true, we can predict the next incident." Roma nodded, "It's a great idea!"

HN overheard the thing.

John suddenly saw him and HN pretended as if he heard nothing. He held an assignment to Roma and said that he would leave. Roma said goodbye and left with John.

John was sure that HN had heard something and feared if he would cause a problem. He left for his house after keeping his documents at a place. That night something unusual happened. While John was sleeping, he heard the opening of his room door. He woke up but found nothing. Again, he heard something but found nothing. He got up and looked around. Suddenly he saw a face with red-eye and screamed. The face disappeared.

"What was that?" he said to himself.

He picked up his phone and called Nelmon. It was raining outside and it was midnight, Nelmon had difficulty coming to his house.

"This isn't fair! I was having a lovely sleep!" Nelmon said.

"I'm sorry but I had to!" John said.

He explained everything to Nelmon. He was surprised. He couldn't get that why would someone with an unusual appearance come to John's house.

In a moment they had a call from the office and it said that John's cabin had been robbed.

"What the hell!" John grabbed his coat and with Nelmon went to the office.

The cabin's condition itself explained that it had been robbed. The documents lay haphazardly on the floor.

The drawers were left open and so were the lockers.

"The parcel has been robbed!" John said in disappointment.

"I told you to look at the proof and not pay attention to who send it!" Nelmon said.

"I'm sorry!" John said.

"Look, there's a letter for you!" Nelmon looked at a letter on the table. He opened it and read,

"I gave you one chance to look at the proof
And you lost it. You paid attention to my
Identity and not to the proof. It went according
To what I had planned. Isn't it interesting, John!
So, let me tell you who I am.

I AM THE ONE BEHIND ALL THESE ATTACKS!
You can call me a Psycho!"
Nelmon and John looked at each other. "Psycho!"

5

INCERTITUDE

In the morning the whole office was dazed by the robbery. Roma came with HN. She asked the guard officer about what had happened.

John looked at HN and felt unusual. Something in his appearance kept him thinking.

"I think I've seen someone like him," thought John. His lips involuntarily spelled out a name.

"Psycho"

But John let go of the idea of HN being psycho. There were differences between them. HN seemed a boy of perfectly polite temper, someone who would help anyone. Whether someone asks for help or not.

On the other hand, 'Psycho', as the name suggests, was a maniac of outraging temper. However, both Psycho and HN were intelligent.

John was thinking about it when Meera looked at him.

"You seem in deep thought. You okay," she said.

"Yes, I am," John replied.

"So, what were you thinking?"

"Oh, where would you love to go after we're married?"

Meera looked with a surprised expression, "seriously!"

"You can take it easy, don't worry!" John left and went to Nelmon. Meera was confused.

"Has he come here to solve the case or marry me?"

Nelmon asked the same question to John about his thought. John explained his incertitude. Meera was listening and she said,

"Really?"

"Oh, Meera. I'm really confused. What place do you really like? I'm looking upon us getting married!"

Meera glared and left irritated.

"Nice one!" Nelmon said

"Thank you!"

HN approached them and asked, "How're you two doing?"

"We're fine!" Nelmon replied. "Who are you?"

"I'm HN. Roma's friend and teacher," HN replied.

"Wow!" Nelmon was surprised by the answer.

"I know you too, HN," John replied.

He saw HN's face carefully and the face he had seen last night came into his mind. But he again shook the idea off his brain. This idea occurred many a time in his brain during the moment he was talking to HN.

"John! John!" HN called.

"Ye- Ye- Yes," John came to senses and bid goodbye. He went to his cabin and lay down on the couch.

He closed his eyes and put all the data in order inside his brain and started clearly thinking. After a moment, he got up and wrote all points he thought of:

- Jake didn't escape himself, someone helped him.
- The truck/car collisions were caused by someone.
- The plane crash was caused by someone.
- The government official car attack was caused by someone.
- The attacks after these also were caused by someone.
- This someone calls himself "Psycho".
- HN may be or may not be.

John now had to actually analyze Roma's book. If that person had powers, it was probably killing people with his eye.

News reached the USCRI (United States Committee for Refugees and Immigrants) headquarters in Washington D.C that a ship carrying migrants from Iraq was found empty on the shores with the officers on board dead. The migrants were not there. The police arrived at the scene to examine. John also was there.

The officers on board lay dead with gunshots on their bodies.

"This is unusual, sir. Why would the migrants kill the officers and escape?" asked Mc Ornald Dezeo, a member of USCRI and the one who looked after the number of migrants who arrived.

"No, sir no. The migrants haven't done anything but someone who goes by the name Psycho has done it," said John.

"Who's Psycho?" Mr. Dezeo asked

"Can't say, but he may be the real culprit."

Mrs. Debbie was informed about the incident and she lay over her concerns about the ongoing situations in America. She ordered that a meeting will be held with the President in the White House. Next week Monday was the day decided for the meeting.

While this was being deceived, John was scrutinizing the area for the sake of finding at least one cue. To his sure shock, he saw something written with chalk, but again the words were not clear. It was a combination of words and symbols that read as "|| is *|.| |\/: |:"

John copied the written message and looked at it with deep thought. Then he mused for a second.

He called an officer and told him to take this note and give it to Roma. Then he asked to tell her to hand over the note to HN.

Roma came to John and asked,

"Why do

you want me to give this note to HN."

"For some reason."

"Ok."

While John remained at the site of the episode, Roma went to HN to hand over the note.

She reached near a flat. A man thick mustache and naked head approached her and asked in a deep, heavy voice,

"How may I help you, young lady?"

"Where is HN Maaki living?"

"Room no 33, 3rd floor."

Roma went to the provided address. She knocked on the door and a girl opened it.

"Yes, please?" she asked.

"Does HN Maaki live here?" Roma asked.

"Of course, come in," the girl led Roma in and called HN.

He came out of a small cabin in the corner and smiled at Roma.

"How're you here?" he asked.

"I came to give a note John wanted you to read." Roma handed over the note to HN. The girl there said, "I'll leave, HN."

"Goodbye, take care."

Roma turned to the door to leave but stopped.

"Who was the girl?" she asked.

"She works here with her father. She studies law. So do I. so we both study here together. I think you might have met her father, the bald mustache man," HN replied,

"Yes, yes I did. I asked him about your address."

After this, Roma left.

HN opened the note and looked at it carefully.

John was eagerly waiting for the letter to come. He looked at the door every now and then, expecting a postman. His patience was gifted when a man holding a letter and a note came to him.

"John? A letter for you," the man said.

"Thanks, John maybe me!" John took the letter and opened it. The note with it was his for sure but the letter wasn't from HN. It belonged to someone else. Also, it wasn't about his note. It was about something else.

John read the letter,

Dear sir,

The president has been, for some days, getting anonymous calls. These calls were very depressing for the president and he quit doing all his work. He sat in his room roaming around the balcony waiting for another call. Yesterday, a letter came to him and a note was attached to it. The letter told us to give the note to you. And it told the President to cancel the meeting with the FBI. We want you to provide safety to him.

Secretary of the president,
Joser Pansen

John was shocked. It wasn't his note according to the letter but he knew it was his. If he had sent the letter to HN, how did it went to the president? He was thinking when HN came running to him.

"John, your note!" he called.

"MY note?" John looked surprised.

"Yes, the one you sent me!" HN replied.

"But I got it back."

"No! Now you'll get it back."

"Then what is this?" John held out the note he had got a moment back and compared it with one HN gave.

"This can't be! Who could have copied my note without looking at it?" John said.

"I don't get it? What and who?"

"I gave you the note and I get the same one from the President who says it was anonymous. If my real note was with you, how did this someone copy it?" John explained.

"OK, someone is playing with you."

"I know who."

"Who?"

"I won't say. Anyways, thank you."

John left with both the notes and sat in his room, confused. For the next two hours, he looked at the notes carefully trying to find at least one flaw, one difference. When nothing turned up, he surrendered.

Meera entered and found John in deep stress.

"You okay?" Meera asked.

"No, and I'm serious this time. Someone is playing with me. I found a half-written message on the ship and copied it on a note. I sent it to HN, expecting an answer. I did get it but after I get the same note from the President with a letter. How is this possible? Without the person looking at the note, he copies it. And these two notes seem the same. I don't know which one is mine," John said.

For the first time, John expressed the actual worry to Meera.

"Give me the notes and the notebook whose page you used to write the note."

Meera looked at the notes carefully and smiled.

"John! This one is yours. The other note doesn't belong to this paper. The color of the fake note's paper is dimmer than the actual."

John hopped out of his chair in excitement.

"I'm really a big fool, why didn't I think of it?"

"Now you accept you're a fool!" Meera said.

"Aw! You look so cute!"

Meera glared and left.

Now John paid attention to the answer. It said,

"His eyes were red."

To John, it was clear that Psycho had used red-eye to kill people. But he had to make it clear to the other people involved in the case, especially Mrs. Debbie.

Roma picked her phone to call HN. He didn't answer and she called again. HN didn't answer any call at all.

"What's wrong with him? Why isn't he answering?" she thought.

With no option left, Roma grabbed her bag and left for HN's house. She found the girl, whom HN studied, outside of the building.

"Is HN home or not?" Roma inquired.

"Yes, he's at home," the girl replied.

"Thanks!"

Roma knocked at HN's home door and no one opened the door.

She hang up the bell and still, no one opened it. She felt worried, so she called the mustached man for help. With two more persons, they smashed open the door. The room was in a state of total devastation. There were blood drops at some points. When they checked the whole room, Roma suddenly opened the small cabin and found HN lying totally injured on the floor.

"HN!" Roma went to him and held him on her knees. The police were called immediately and so was called the doctor. HN was shifted to the hospital and the police started to examine the whole room.

While in hospital, Roma called John and told him everything. John was shocked, He thought that Psycho might have attacked him. He reached the hospital in a jiffy. Roma was waiting there.

"What happened?" John Asked.

"HN was attacked. He is in serious condition," Roma said.

"It's all my fault. Why did I involve him in this case?"

John was sure that Psycho had attacked HN and it was all because he had given HN the note to solve.

"Or did Psycho attack HN because he's with Roma!" thought John.

6

BATTLE OF THE NOUS

At the beginning of this chapter, I can clearly say that by now the two most intelligent persons are poles apart standing against each other. Where on the side of the Americans and the FBI we have John. On the other side, we have Psycho. These two witty brains are no less than each other. The only thing that separates them is their way of judgment and shrewdness.

John was standing outside of the hospital waiting for Nelmon to come. He arrived soon.

"Well, what is the news today?" he asked.

"HN was found injured in his room when Roma went to meet him," John said.

"Really! I know you'll be thinking that Psycho has done it all."

"Yes! I don't know why."

"Where's Roma?"

"She's in the room with HN."

"OK!"

Nelmon went to see Roma and HN. When he reached into the hospital area, he found Roma at the medical shop buying some medicines. He went to her and asked,

"You okay, Roma? How's HN?"

"I'm fine and HN is okay. Just some injuries they'll heal," Roma replied.

"That's some good news!"

Both Nelmon and Roma went to see HN's condition. He was injured badly. There were scars wounds on every part of his body. His shirt was torn off. John also came in and looked at HN's situation. Inside he was broken and thought why he involved HN in this case. But suddenly something came in thought. HN was holding a note in his hand, tightly. John got it out and saw it,

"Look, John! This Battle of the Nous is between you and me. Either you win or I. But if you involve anyone else in this battle, excluding the FBI, That person is going to die! So John shall we begin…"

John was furious and he, slamming the door, went out. Nelmon and Roma looked in surprise.

"What happened to him?" Nelmon said.

"I don't know?"

John returned to the office and went to his cabin.

"Why am I being fooled every time!"

He threw things on the floor and cried out loud.

Meera heard him and came to see him.

"What's the matter? Why are you like this?" She asked.

"I'm being fooled by a Psycho. Someone who doesn't do anything normally is fooling a normal witty brain," John replied.

"You are again thinking too much John. This is what he wants. He is doing everything like a normal brain but he knows you will think everything and won't check the basics."

"I don't get you?"

"He is playing like an amateur and expects you to think he is mature."

John was blocked. He couldn't get anything the first time but when he understood it, he was shocked.

"Then I'm a big fool!"

"Yes, you are!"

Meera replied and John answered with a smile.

Roma sat with HN till night because he had no one to take care of. She called Tee to tell her that she would stay.

At last, HN woke up and looked around.

"HN! Thank God! You're okay," Roma said.

"I don't remember coming here," HN said softly.

"Because you were unconscious. Could you tell us what happened?"

"I was studying in my cabin when I heard my flower pot break. When I came out to see, someone hit me on my head. Then when I got up I tried to call the police, but the person held me and we fought. I couldn't hold him and he attacked me with a knife. Then I went unconscious."

Listening to his story, Roma thought that now she could confirm that everything was happening according to her book. She called John to tell him HN was conscious. John said that he would come to meet him in a moment.

"But before that, I would look upon the migrant case," he said.

He went to the office of USCRI to ask them about the migrants. It was late evening when he reached there.

"Hello, Sir! Could I possibly get some information about the trip?" Mr. Dezeo asked.

"What, please?" John asked.

Mr. Dezeo explained that the only stop the ship made was at London. But no stranger was seen going on board. Still, the migrants were gotten off the ship and the officers were killed.

"This is awkward. Still thank you. See you tomorrow."

John left and reached his house.

John sat in comfort trying to forget everything that happened today. But his peace was interrupted when his bell rang. He opened the door and found no one. Before he could close the door, the bell rang again.

"John, it's me, Nelmon,"

John let him in and close the door.

"Why were you doing this?" John asked

"Doing what?" Nelmon said.

"You rang the bell the first and then you hid."

"No, I just arrived."

"Then did you see anyone else outside."

"Yes, a man in a dark outfit. He was waiting for you outside."

John went out that very moment and caught the man. The man said nothing and held out a parcel to him. John held it, while the man ran. He came in with the parcel and wrapped it. Both Nelmon and John took interest in the parcel. They curiously opened it and discovered a bunch of pieces of paper. They looked at them and found nothing written.

"It's a joke!" John said.

"Who played it on us?" Nelmon said.

"Probably Psycho!"

Mrs. Debbie was in her office with her niece who had to go to a violin playing competition. Mrs. Debbie loved her niece more than anyone so she sent Meera with her to the competition.

"Are you good at playing the violin?" Meera asked.

"Yes! I am!" Mrs. Debbie's niece said.

While on way someone attacked them. The someone was Psycho.

Meera tried to save Mrs. Debbie's niece, Cathy but failed she went unconscious and Psycho took Cathy. After a moment, Mrs. Debbie had a call from him.

"If you want your niece to be safe, do like the way I say." Mrs. Debbie was shocked. She left helpless. She called Meera and no one picked up. She waited and after a while, Meera's call came but someone else was calling.

"The girl you're calling is in hospital. Any message you want to leave."

Mrs. Debbie hung up and went to John to tell him that Meera had been attacked.

When John got to know he was furious.

"Whoever did this, I'm gonna kill him! Definitely!" He said.

Mrs. Debbie looked at him thinking if she should convey the message. But couldn't risk her niece's life. So she said nothing but she at least said that maybe during the attack on Meera, Cathy might've been there.

However, John was too deep in the thought of saving Meera that he couldn't get the message,

Mrs. Debbie was left her heartbroken. Now she had to do everything the kidnapper said to save Cathy. John on the other hand worried with the thought that whether Meera was alright or not and remained in his cabin. He had decided to take a big leap to catch Psycho. He decided not to be fooled by him again. Also, it was clear to him that it won't be easy not to be fooled by Psycho. After all, he wasn't normal, he was a maniac.

"Gosh! How could anyone live with such a maniac!" he thought.

Yes, it isn't easy to live with a psycho but they're humans too and they have a right to live too. They are no different from us. All they've different is a too desperate way of thinking or looking at the world.

So I can say that this Psycho in this book also has a long painful story in his life. He was struggled to live in this non-harmonious world.

"I wonder what this world is? Hell or Heaven. I lived in one milieu and was brought to another society. I didn't change, but my surroundings changed. I died like a tropical flower brought in a cold place."
-Psycho.

8 years ago:
Psycho was a twelve-year-old boy who lived in Japan with his parents. His dad was called upon for some work in America. His mom was an American, so the family decided to shift to America. But Psycho had one little problem. He wasn't good at speaking English; he was weak at it. His mom had tried her best to teach him English, but he wasn't willing to learn. When the decision of going to America was taken, Psycho refused to go there. His parents tried to motivate him, but he didn't listen to them. His father somehow brought him to say yes. Soon the family left for America. Psycho was admitted to a local school. But he faced a lot of problems. He was bullied now and then and he couldn't complain about it to anyone. His life was a punishment for him and he wasn't able to stop it. For four years he lived a miserable life. But he had a superb level of patience. He tolerated everything until one day.
He returned from school and called his parents. They said that they'd return by eight o'clock. So, he thought of waiting for them to have dinner. But his parents didn't come. The clock reached 08:15 PM and he grew impatient for the first time. He called but no one picked up. Then, police arrived to meet him. He started feeling unsecured. The police said that his parents died in an accident and that they'd have to take him into custody.
Psycho, however, didn't let them take him. He said they would show him his parents and then only he would let them

take him. The police refused to say that they were under investigation. Psycho didn't believe them and kept saying them to let him meet his parents. When none responded, he threw a heavy stone at one of the officers. Other officers quickly held Psycho and put him in the car saying, "He's a maniac! Take him to the asylum."

He was made unconscious and taken to the mental asylum. His miserable life didn't seem to have any end. Again, for four years he lived like a dying person who has no will to live.

However, he had something very powerful. He was amazingly intelligent. So, he could easily fool a normal average brain, something which helped him escape the asylum.

On one such regular Thursday night, when the patients were being shifted from one place to another, news came that the asylum from which the patients came was badly on fire. The buses carrying the patients stopped at a point for rest. The drivers got off and had dinner. There were four of them and they were in the restaurant when one of them said, "Hey, Ron, Look. The back door of your bus is open!"

When they reached to see, one of the patients was missing. It was Psycho.

The police were called, but they couldn't figure out which patient had escaped. The numbers allotted to patients were missing from their shirts.

The police searched the adjacent areas but found none. Now they asked for information from the hospital. Unfortunately, the whole hospital and accompanying offices were set on fire which had let to the loss of all the information. This thing looked like a setup. But whoever had done that, was unknown.

Four officers, namely officers Black, Norman, Jean & Russo were given the responsibility of finding the escaped patient.

The officers searched the adjacent areas of the site of escape till around 4 A.M. At that time, when the officers were giving the last round check, something happened. Three of the officers heard a scream.

"Black! It's you?" Norman cried.

While two of the officers went to search, the officer's left-back saw red-eye in the shadows and screamed. The other two officers met the same fate.

The next morning the death of the four officers was the headline. Ever after that day, Psycho never came in front of the whole world. Also, neither the Japanese government nor the American government took the responsibility for him and the death of his family. He was lost for a long time until the Pod DC hotel shooting or PDCHC.

John grabbed his car key and drove off to the hospital to meet Roma. But when he reached there, he saw something happening. People had gathered around. A man, totally masked and covered, held HN on the top of the building. He had a gun in his hand. Roma stood in the group below, feeling helpless. John ran to her and she explained everything in one breath.

"Don't worry! I'll find a way to save him," John said.

John went up stealthily to save HN. But when he reached the door leading to the top, he found it was closed. He called Nelmon immediately to help him. Until Nelmon reached, John need to ensure that nothing happened to HN.

So, Roma kept an eye on the incident. She kept informing John about what was happening. Nelmon arrived quickly and both of them broke the door. At that very moment, the man slipped and fell from the building. HN came on his knees. Shivering and crying. John held him quickly and Roma also came there. The nurses were called and the man was shifted to the hospital. HN was brought down and taken to the FBI office.

"This is going too far! I've ruined HN's life!" John said

"No, John! It's not your fault!" Roma said and Nelmon agreed.

"Then what do you think this is? His fate or my mistake!" John said.

Roma turned towards HN and said, "He told me, it's never one's mistake, it's always fate."

"Fine! Let's call this his fate. But fate doesn't repeat itself!" John slammed the door going out.

Roma and Nelmon again felt awkward over John's behavior. He had done the same thing when he had found the letter in HN's hand while he was admitted.

"Why does he act like this?" Nelmon said.

John went to his house and called Mrs. Debbie to ask about Meera. She said that she was alright and would be coming back soon. This thing comforted John a little bit. However, he had been totally worried about Meera but now he was tensed due to HN's situation. John thought over this a little bit. He tried to use common sense to break through this situation. It worked. He could get an idea that something was wrong in whatever happened until now. If HN had been attacked then the attacker would have killed him at the very moment and even if he had got to know that someone was coming he should have taken HN with him. He would have not left him to let Roma and others know that HN was being hunted. It looked as if HN or maybe Psycho wanted John to know HN was being hunted. It was clear that at some point in the story HN appeared to be Psycho for John. But more than half of the story expressed that HN was nowhere near Psycho. John left frustrated.

"If I consider HN as Psycho, then my case is done but if I don't then it gets deeper and deeper," thought John. He kept thinking for half of the night.

HN woke up in the middle of the night while he heard a scream. Roma was sleeping on the couch near HN's bed.

"Roma! Get up!" he said.

She opened her eyes and yawned.

"What's the…matter?"

"I heard a scream!" HN said worryingly.

"I didn't."

"I did. I'm not feeling good here. I want to go back home."

"Now now! Now sleep. Don't worry."

While Roma was comforting HN, they heard another scream. That time it was loud.

Both Roma and HN came out to see what had happened. Two people came out of a room holding the dead body of a nurse. She was dead and had deep wounds and injuries.

Roma asked what had happened and the two persons said that they heard a scream and came running to see what had happened. They found the poor soul dead.

"That's not good. I'll call the police." Roma called the police and then called John. HN went back to the bed for rest and slept in a moment. Roma also came in a while and waited for John.

The next morning it was raining but good for HN that he was discharged from the hospital. He went to Roma's home with her.

John, on the other hand, wasn't in a very good mood. He went to meet Meera. She was in Mrs. Debbie's office.

"Meera! You okay?" he asked.

"Yes, I'm fine thanks for your concern. I just would want to say to you that an unusual-looking guy attacked Cathy. Mrs.

Debbie says that Cathy is safe and sound. I don't know how she remained safe. There is something wrong, John," Meera said.

"I think you're right. Not only that, something's wrong with what had happened with HN. I think both are related to Psycho.

7

Nival of Blood

John was in his home having cessation from all thoughts until now. He was trying to relax. No doubt when you are against someone who is certifiable, you want to take a breath. But John didn't have this in his fate. Someone came to hand him a letter. It was an official letter from the Indian ambassador in the US.

The letter said that the Indian Ambassador would be taking the US ambassador to India for a trip and to meet with the Prime Minister. He would be expecting protection from some of the trained officials in the FBI for the ongoing bloody situation in the US. John called Mrs. Debbie but she didn't pick up. So, he called Meera to inform her about this.

Mrs. Debbie couldn't help possibly. After all her niece was at the brink of her life. If Mrs. Debbie took any wrong step her niece would breathe her last. She couldn't let this happen possibly. She had to, in return for her niece, give the kidnapper something. This was the timing and place of the meeting between the US ambassador and the Prime Minister. Mrs. Debbie had to do this. She went to the Indian Ambassador's office to meet her. Divya Patel, the Indian Ambassador, welcomed Mrs. Debbie happily with a nice heart-warming congenial hug. She sat by her side and said, "How may I help you?"

"I've come here to gather information about the meeting of Mr. Jeremy Octane with the Indian Prime Minister," Mrs. Debbie replied.

"Ok. It might be about the security of Mr. Octane. I did send a letter to John about this."

"You did. That's great. So, I might take the information."

Divya got up and pulled a file out of a bunch of books.

"This is very important keep it safe."

Mrs. Debbie took the file and went away quickly. She called the kidnapper to tell him that she has got the files and needed to meet him immediately.

"Meet me at Capital One Arena to hand over the files. Don't think I'll leave your niece that easily," the kidnapper said.

"I'm coming! What!" Mrs. Debbie hung up and left for Capital One Arena.

The stadium was at a three minutes distance.

When Mrs. Debbie reached the stadium, a guy in a black outfit and a mask was waiting.

"The file!" the guy said.

"My niece!" Mrs. Debbie demanded.

"Not until I don't do my work."

"But," Mrs. Debbie said.

"No, buts hand over me the file!"

Mrs. Debbie handed over the file but stopped before completely transferring it.

"No. I won't give you the file." She said.

She turned and tried to run but the guy shot her in the leg and she fell.

The guy came to her and looked into her eyes.

"Fine!"

Mrs. Debbie saw a red dot and breath her last.

***

The whole arrangement was made for the coming of the US Ambassador to India. He was to stay in the Shangri-La's Eros Hotel in Delhi. The hotel was beautifully set up for the visit of the Ambassador. Nothing was kept untouched. The Indian Foreign Minister was at the airport waiting for the US Ambassador, to welcome him. The Ambassador reached around 05:00 Pm IST (06:30 Am EST). He was given a warm welcome and taken to his destination.

But he was unknown of all the dangers he was about to face. He had a nice drive up to his hotel.

John also had come to India. He was staying in the same hotel as the Ambassador. He had to ensure that the Ambassador remained sage and no danger in the name of Psycho came.

Back in America, Meera had searched the whole office for Mrs. Debbie but there was no sign of her anywhere. Not even her phone was working.

"Where is Mrs. Debbie!" thought Meera.

She called her home but her householder said that she hadn't been home since the last day. That thing put Meera in worry. She asked about Mrs. Debbie's niece and the householder that she also had not been home since her audition. Meera hung up quickly and called John to tell him but he didn't pick up. Probably he was busy.

Meera started to feel worried. She had no one to contact and tell. Not even Nelmon. Now she was left with only one option, to call Roma. She called her and told her about everything.

"What! I'm coming to meet you right now!" Roma said. She came quickly to meet Meera.

With no highly ranked FBI officer to help them, Roma and Meera thought of finding Mrs. Debbie on their own.

Back in India, John kept a close eye on the Ambassador who was having a meeting with the Indian PM. Nothing was supposed to go wrong.

The Ambassador was sitting beside a Minister. Suddenly a bullet passed directly in front of the Ambassador and the wall. The bullet was meant to kill the Ambassador but the shot was missed.

The whole cabin rushed around in panic. The bullet was fired again and it hit the Minister who was seated beside the Ambassador. He died the very moment. While the panicked cabin came out, a blast happened outside the building and many reporters and local people died and some were injured. These two things happened simultaneously and suddenly, giving no time to recover. Ambulances reached and so did the police and army. The injured were being shifted to the hospital quickly as fast as possible. The news was aired live and Roma was watching. She called John but his phone came busy.

One of the news reported that the Minister who died was the Defense Minister. But it was not confirmed yet. Roma was called to go to India and report about the situation now. It was because the Indian reporter for CNN was injured.

She was taken there quickly, though she reached there the next day.

The investigation was underway in New Delhi where this incident took place. But the search couldn't cinch who the dead minister was because the building had collapsed and the dead could not be identified.

Roma met John, who was with the US Ambassador who was injured. They were in the hospital. Roma looked at the TV which was having the headlines aired when the airing was interrupted abruptly.

"We have a message for the people. A guy has given this communiqué to tell you about this."

All of a sudden, a person covered started to speak. That was being broadcasted around the world.

"I want to introduce myself. I am Psycho. I may tell you, this is your world and it does not belong to these politicians or government officials who burglarize you and leave you with hopes that are lies and nothing. They live there lifelong and don't even care whether you live or die. They ask for taxes and money, even from the poorest of the poor. Underdeveloped countries are not because of their people but because of these greedy, avaricious, and gluttonous rich people. Don't let them ruin your world.

I was in affliction because of them. They didn't want me but I'll make them feel my need. Who are they! Gods! No! No! No! They're just humans like you all. But they just make themselves different because of more money. They are surrounded by guards for they fear they'll die and when they die the whole world is forced to mourn. But when a poor person dies of hunger no one ever gets to know. Some so many poor people have perished around the world and no one has ever mourned their death.

We call ourselves humans! Right! Are you real humans? Ask yourself this question! Ask it! Now! What answer do you have? These rich, criminal people force us to not act like a human. No. Don't do this! Start acting like humans. Don't let them steal from you your reward.

Enough is enough! I want all of you to join me in a worldwide protest against our government leaders. Do not let them crack up our world. Fight! Fight!"

The channels went off for a moment and then came back. Roma looked at John and said, "What the heck is he thinking? He is a psycho!"

"Can I ask you something Roma? Did you leave HN on his own or with, your sister?" asked John.

"On his own. Why are you asking?"

"Just something. I'll be back."

John went outside of the hospital and called the FBI headquarters. He told them to keep an eye on HN for 1 week or so and report back to him.

"Even if I have this ambiguity, I should clear it at once," he said to himself.

The report of the dead came in the evening. Estimated 23 people had died and 28 were injured, out of which 5 were critical. John at once visited the Delhi Police Headquarters for the report.

Mrs. Shilpa Chaudry was the working commissioner and she was heading the investigation of the case. She welcomed John and handed over him the report. It contained the names of the victims, both dead and injured, some photos, and information about the incident.

"This didn't appear to be a terrorist attack to me." Mrs. Shilpa said.

"I know it's not a one and I have a reason for that," John said.

"What?"

"A guy who calls himself Psycho has done this. Because he threatens to destroy this world balance of good and bad. Like we know access to everything is bad. If there is too much good in this world it won't probably work out for us, not even in the case of too much bad."

"This Psycho is the person who addressed live on TV. Isn't he?"

"Yes!"

"He is a Psycho!"

Their meeting was interfered with by a knock with a heavy voice behind.

"A parcel of the investigation for Mrs. Shilpa Chaudary."

Shilpa opened the door and brought the parcel in. She opened the file and read it. After a moment, when she was done with reading, she looked at John. He found her to be near a agape like ajar.

"What's wrong? Anything special?" asked John.

"Yes. This is something very special. The shooter has been seen on the camera. We can capture him!" Shilpa said.

She left at an instant and John held the parcel to analyze it. He dug a little deeper into the situation and found that there was more in-depth than at the top. We cannot raven for treasure on the official. It's always waiting at the meat-and-potatoes.

When John saw the parcel, he found a paper on which an eye was drawn and he could get the meaning correctly.

This parcel was not for the Delhi Police, but John. Psycho knows everything." John thought.

This thought was a little awkward. How come he knows everything without being around. Something was seriously wrong. John called one of the officers who he had sent to follow HN.

John called one of the officers who he had sent to follow HN.

"Hello! Crane!" John said.

"Hello, John!" a familiar voice answered.

"Is it you Crane?"

"Yes! John, it's me!"

"Look, I think you should stay a little away from HN. I doubt he's Psycho!"

"Hahahaha! As if you never could understand who I am!"

"Psycho!"

"Yes, Yes! Crane just went to heavens!"

"You criminal?"

"No need to say. I know who I am."

"I am going to leave but it doesn't mean that I am falling back!"

"Who is this HN? I did try to kill him last time but it was just a warning for you. This time I expect to eliminate him.

Psycho hung up soon and John panicked and called Roma to tell her that HN's life was in danger.

Meera arrived in Japan and directly went to the National Police Agency (NPA) headquarters in Chiyoda, Tokyo.

She went to the office of the Chief Inspector. She was a lady in her thirties but young and charming. Her face lied about her age. She was wearing a blue outfit with a badge on her breast pocket telling her name. Her eyes contrasted with her outfit. She welcomed Meera with a smile.

"Hiomi Kaya, Chief Inspector, NPA," She said.

"I'm Meera Saaki. Head of local police in D.C, USA and a working officer of FBI."

"So what has brought you here?

"I came here to discuss something important. Some 8 years ago a Maaki family shifted to America when their son was twelve. But when he was 14, his mother and father died in a car accident. Could you somehow get me his name," Meera said.

"Let me check the data. Until then would you like to have something?" Hiromi asked.

"No, thanks!"

Hiromi went through some data and found three files of cases about the Maaki family. One case was of fraud and the other about murder. But one set at all conditions which Meera said.

"Look, here it is," Hiromi showed Meera the file.

The father's name was Hibiki Maaki, mother's name war Arty Maaki and the son's name was HN Maaki or Hironaga Maaki.

"HN Maaki!" Meera jumped off her seat and immediately called John to tell him her discovery.

John was shocked to know the information. It was a very big surprise for him.

Roma, on the other side, had left for America. She was dead worried about HN, praying for him to be okay. She called Tee to ask her about HN. Roma, before leaving, had told HN to visit Tee in case she needed anything. So, she could at least tell whether he was okay or not.

"Tee! Did HN visit you?" Roma said.

"No. He didn't but uncle Josh did. He was asking about you. He said he wanted to meet you," Tee replied.

"Was it important?"

"I think. He was looking a little worried when I said you weren't here."

"Listen. Go and visit HN's home and remember don't go alone. Take Milan with you."

Tee took her friend Milan and went to see HN. His home door was locked.

"Probably he isn't home," Milan said.

"I'll call Roma," Tee said.

She was about to call Roma When HN came.

"Hello, Tee. How're you?" he said.

"Hi, HN. Roma told me to visit you," Tee said.

"I'm sorry for not visiting you. I had promised her that I'd. But I had to put up some assignments for the class, so I was busy."

"No big deal! She was just worried; I'd be better to talk to her and tell her you're okay."

"I will."

HN took out his phone and called Roma but her phone was switched off.

"I think she's busy," HN said.

"She might be in the plane. Don't worry," Tee said.

"I'll call her when she reaches or just come to meet her."

Tee and Milan left their respective ways.

HN's phone rang and he picked it up.

"Meera Saaki went to Japan. She knows everything about you," the caller said.

"Doesn't matter. At least she never will know that I'm…"

8

PHANTOM OF PERPLEXITY

"Doesn't matter. At least she never will know that I'm PSYCHO!" HN said.

Roma's uncle, Uncle Josh, heard him and was about to leave when HN caught him.

"I don't like to kill innocent people. So, when they get to know my truth I kind of make them suicide." HN said.

"No! please! I beg you to say to leave me. I won't tell anyone. If you probably leave my niece, please," Uncle Josh said.

"I can't. I kind of have an affection for her. I'm just addicted to her. I love her!"

HN took away uncle Josh and brought him under his control.

John arrived in America just after Roma did. He first visited her. When he reached her house he found many people who were crying. Roma was in a black outfit with HN beside her.

"What happened Roma?" John asked.

"My uncle!" Roma Cried.

"What? Is he okay?" John said.

"Roma's uncle committed suicide,' HN replied

"That's not good at all! I feel for you, Roma."

Roma was sniveling, her heartbroken. HN held her hand and said, "Please hold yourself. I can't see you crying like that. It hurts me!"

Roma hugged him the moment he said it.

"Please don't leave me in my grief!" she said.

"I won't! ever!"

Tee also came to comfort her sister. John stood in the corner thinking of this situation which was not exhortative. It just came suddenly without warning. It wasn't good for Roma at all.

"I just don't feel that HN is right for Roma. He is a good boy though but I don't feel Roma is secured around him," John thought, "Oh she is excessively secured!"

That evening nobody was happy for Roma's family including Roma. John was worried about Roma. If Psycho killed her uncle, he could also kill Roma.

But his mind just turned around and he started thinking about Meera.

"I should call her to know when she will be coming," thought John but he suddenly remembered that he had to meet Mrs. Debbie. He was really expeditious in changing and then going to meet Mrs. Debbie, although she wasn't there or anywhere. When he arrived at the headquarters, he found off junior officers outside accompanied by some forensic officers. Soon a body was brought outside. It was covered in a sheet, so John couldn't see who it was.

He went to one of the officers and inquired who it was. "Mrs. Debbie, Sir," the officer replied.

John was shocked and came to the end of his unit. He just couldn't believe it. He went inside the office and asked one of the senior officers.

"Well, when we came up in the morning to meet Mrs. Debbie, we found her lying on the couch in her office. She was dead when we examined her," the officer said.

"How's this possible?" John asked.

"Don't know, sir.

John quickly called Meera.

"You're saying this now. Where were you when I called you to tell that Mrs. Debbie is not under my contact anymore, that I can't find where she is!" Meera said.

"I'm sorry! I might've been busy!" John said.

"Busy? Never mind! You're careless!" Meera hung up with a voice that said she was crying.

John stood for a little time and he became tearful. His eyes moisten, and he took a deep breath. He left for home, heartbroken. On the way, when he found himself at the metro station, his eyes caught a person in a hooded upper; a cap and mask. He looked like the person whom John saw in the footage of the camera of the criminal block.

"Psycho!" John said.

Before he could start following him, a metro crossed by the very moment.

"No, No, No," John tried to find a way to follow him. When the train fully passed. John jumped to the other platform, where Psycho was standing a moment ago. There were a lot of people and John couldn't track his prey. However soon his prey had entered his vision and he followed him up to the mall. Psycho entered a crowded ally and John found it difficult to keep his footsteps. But he kept on following him no matter what hurdles came. For a moment Psycho disappeared from the crowd and John tried to look around in haste. Suddenly, when he turned around towards the dead-end of the ally, he came face to face with Psycho. There was a moment of pause. Neither of the two did anything.

"You're Psycho?" said John.

"Yes," he replied.

John couldn't believe his eyes when he saw Psycho's eye, the red eye. Nothing until now had been a lie. Roma was right. Psycho had powers!

But John soon collapsed and suffered a blackout.

"It was a long way up to here," Psycho whispered in the ear, John.

When John opened his eyes he saw a doctor examining him and Meera standing near the door of the room.

"He's back, at last," the doctor.

"John!" Meera came and hugged him.

"What happened? I don't get anything," John said.

"You were unconscious for three days. I became worried. The doctor said you were alive but not in sense," Meera said.

"What? Really!" John said, bewildered of what his conditions had been.

"Yes. I didn't tell anything about the incidents which have taken place to Roma."

"Good. She's already in the status quo of the passing away of her uncle. Which isn't good for a young girl like her. She can't entertain much of the proceeding which has taken place."

"I acquiesce your word of concern for Roma."

Nelmon entered in the very instant and asked the condition of John.

"I find myself in a fine fettle," John said.

"Could you explain now, what took place three days ago with you in the ally?" Nelmon said.

"I met my repugnant enemy. Someone I don't like at all," John replied.

"You mean Psycho," said Meera.

"Yes! He has powers. No some simple joke or dynamism. Supernatural powers," John said.

"What did he do?" Meera said.

"I looked into his red eye and lost my senses. I can't bethink the affair," replied John.
"What you said is enough clue for us to know Psycho has powers," said Nelmon.
The three sat trying to get rid of the fancy that they can't catch the lawless and felonious con.
Roma was in her room, reminding herself of all her anamnesis when Tee entered in. She had brought coffee for her sister.
"Roma, it's good-for-nothing you thinking about the death of Uncle Josh. It's down memory lane. You need to blink it and leave it," she said.
"I know. But I can't help myself musing about whatever has taken place. I have taken the count. I've lost to the life, totally," Roma said.
"No, you haven't. You still are in the battle. You need to fight."
Roma gave a smile and said,
"You're right! I won't back down easily. Not at all."
The sisters were having an alluring talk when they were held up by HN. He entered the room and smiled at both the sisters.
"HN! Nice to see you," Roma Said.
"I came here to say whether if you're free enough to come out with me? HN said.
"Yes, I'm I might cheer me up."
HN held Roma's hand and took her outside.
"I don't have any car or something. So we can go on a walk," he said.
"I'm okay with that," Roma said.
Both of them walked down the road up to a park. It was nearly saturated with people of different age groups. Roma loved that kind of place. The time of the day had painted

upon a different color in the sky. The sky was azure and the sum's radiance beautified it.

HN and Roma sat near a corner.

"If ever, Roma, you get to know my truth, something you don't want to know, what'll you do?" HN asked.

"I'll cry. The only thing I want is that you don't betray or bite a hand that feeds. I just like you the way you're," Roma said.

HN smiled at Roma and held her hand. He said, "You need not worry. I'm there for you whenever and wherever you need me. Even if I'm not alive."

"Come on, you're being too soft-hearted for me!" Roma said

"No, I'm not."

"No!"

"HN likes me! HN likes me!"

"No, I don't! We're friends!"

"Blah! Blah!"

"No, no, no!"

John was having breakfast in his office when Meera came in. He looked at her and simpered at her.

"What?" she said.

"Do you have any problem if I smile?" John said.

"No. But the way you did smile now wasn't a good one. It was rather kittenish," Meera said.

"Really? That's cute!"

"Anyways, I came here to tell you that the FBI will be voting to decide over a new director."

"Is there anything else than FBI that we can talk about?"

"Yes, like how I should talk about FBI without letting you know about it."

"No! I mean like how great I am. That kind of talk."

"Not interested."

John jumped off his seat and held onto his coat and keys.

"I'll vote, right. No! I've other works to handle. Like if I have to go after a criminal and save America I need to investigate it. Okay!" he said.

"No, you don't get my point. This newly elected director can be in danger from Psycho. He is a criminal, an enemy of the FBI. He can do anything to hurt the FBI," Meera said.

"Doesn't matter for me, now, it's over. Now it's a brawl between Psycho and me, and no one else. Not even FBI."

Meera stood in awe, trying to figure out why John was saying such a thing.

She held his hand and said, "What's gone wrong with you? Why are you acting oddly?"

"I'm not!" John replied.

"Yes, you're don't lie."

"Look, involving you in this thing means putting your life in danger. I don't want such a thing to happen!"

"Belonging to FBI means putting your life in danger for the country. Nothing changes that thing."

"Not in this case, you get it."

"I'm going. I don't want to talk to you!"

Meera left tempestuously, slamming the door.

John couldn't do anything at all. He felt helpless.

Roma and HN returned home and HN then bid goodbye. She entered in and found Nelmon and Meera sitting. Tee was also seated.

"Hello, Meera. Hello, Nelmon," Roma said.

"Hi, Roma! Feeling sorry about your uncle's death." Meera said.

"Hello, Roma," Nelmon said.

"Hi. Thanks for visiting. Did you've something to eat?"

"We're waiting for you for one hour. Where were you?" Meera asked.

"I was with HN. He tried to cheer me up," Roma said.

"Oh! Anyways we came here to invite you to an FBI function for a new director of FBI," Nelmon said.

"Why? What about Mrs. Debbie? Where's she?" Roma asked.

"Roma, we might have bad news for you," Meera said.

"Mrs. Debbie is no more. She is dead," Nelmon said.

"What do you mean by dead?!" Roma said.

"This all was very sudden. We still don't know who killed her or how did she die," Meera said.

"Are you serious?" said Roma

"Yes," Nelmon replied.

Roma burst into tears and Nelmon quickly held her. She couldn't stop crying, while Nelmon tried to comfort her.

"Roma calms down," he said.

"I won't! How can I?" she said.

"Because you have to. You have to remain strong to face this murder," Meera said.

Nelmon held Roma close to him and wiped her tears. He gave her water and said,

"Bravery is not by birth. It's something up to you until you don't want to be brave, you'll never be brave."

Roma held herself a little and took a deep breath. She know Nelmon was right. If Roma had to be brave, she needed to believe in herself and she needed to have the courage of being brave. She had to do this not only for catching Mrs. Debbie's murderer but the murderer of all innocents who he had killed.

"You're right," Roma said.

Nelmon smiled and she answered.

So she got ready for the function. She knew it won't be easy for her but she had to do it.

She planned to take HN with her, so she told him to be ready at around 06:30 P.M.

The function was to be held in Kellogg Conference Hotel. It was a little far from Roma's house but it would work. She and HN reached there around seven in the evening. Nelmon and Mera were waiting. Nelmon was happy to see Roma but when he saw HN with her his smile faded. Meera noticed this and said in a friendly way, "Jealous?"

"Why?"Said Nelmon.

"Just saying. I thought you were jealous because Roma is with HN."

"No!"

"So why did your smile fade away when you saw him?"

"Because John said that he didn't want HN in this party. I forgot to tell Roma not to bring him."

"No worries. He cares a lot and says he doesn't."

Nelmon and Meera went in and joined the couth party. Following that, HN and Roma also came.

"I didn't have to come to her, Roma. I know I'm your friend but I wasn't invited. And it's an FBI official party," HN said.

"No worries! They don't bother," Roma said.

HN looked around. Highly ranked officials having talks and drinks. Food was set up in line with a variety of dishes for options. It looked fabulous but HN hated all these things. He hated the way people showed off their power and money. He took a corner seat and looked around. Nelmon was looking at him continuously.

"Why is he looking around like that?" he thought. HN got up and went towards the washroom. Nelmon followed him.

Nelmon froze at what he was looking at. A truth had been revealed.

"Ps-Psycho!" he said.

Psycho turned around and laughed.

"So what? What are you going to do?" he said.

"HN you are Psycho. I knew it! I'll go and tell everyone!"

"Like who?"

"Roma, John, everyone!"

"I don't know of John but Roma won't believe you."

She will."

"Look it doesn't matter whether they believe or not. Simply, I won't even let you tell them."

"What do you mean by that?" Nelmon asked trembling with fear and shock.

"Kill you. I don't usually kill innocent people but when someone gets to know my truth it's obvious I will eliminate him."

Nelmon was taken aback. He tried to go towards the door but Psycho stopped him.

"Not so easily. Don't you want to know who killed uncle Josh and Mrs. Debbie, her niece, and thousands of people out there?"

Nelmon was in disquietude and started having animosity towards Psycho.

"I killed them all!" HN said in a flagitious manner.

Nelmon held him at his arm and tried to blitz at him but came to naught.

Psycho gave a look and Nelmon saw red-eye and he was ceased to exist.

He fell with a thud and Psycho looked at him. He quickly changed back to HN and gave a loud holler. The whole FBI came on its feet. Roma quickly came and found on the floor Nelmon, dead.

"Nelmon!" Roma said.

"HN, What happened?" Meera said.

"I don't know. I was in the washroom when I heard something. And when I came outside I found him dead," HN replied.

"Did you see someone else?" Meera asked

"No, I didn't. Though I did hear someone else," HN said.

"Voice? What did you hear?" Roma asked.

"Someone was talking about Mrs. Debbie or something like that," HN replied.

"What exactly?" Meera said.

"I couldn't get it clearly because I was rinsing my hands with water and its sound didn't let me hear it," HN said.

"NO problem. Come with me," Meera said.

Meera could smell that something was fishy. It looked as if HN was lying. It was impossible for Nelmon to not scream if someone killed or attacked him. Also, if the killer was Psycho, knowing that someone was in the washroom, Nelmon would have called for help, but according to HN, no such call came. So for Meera to believe HN, there were two possibilities. On that Nelmon didn't know there was someone in the washroom other than he and the killer.

The second possibility was that this killer didn't let Nelmon call for help. Meera kept HN outside and told some officers to keep a look at him. Herself she called John and told him this sad news. John was taken aback. He quickly reached the spot to see his friend one last time. The first time someone's death hurt John the most. He felt like Psycho had done enough. He was now fed up with his existence. Meera came to him and held his hand.

"Have you ever lost someone?" she asked.

"No, not until now," replied John.

"I've lost many including my beloved Exon," Meera said.

"Exon? Who's e?" asked John,

"Someone I loved in my college days. He was a great boy with a nice heart. We had fun during those days. We went to the museum, the beach, the central park, and a lot of many other places."

"Did both of you have the same taste?"

"I was once coming to meet him at a place, our secret one. We got under attack by some goons and they held me. Exon, to save me, let his life at stake."

"He likes you, didn't he?"

"Yes. I don't expect to find such love again. Never."

"I think you should."

"And who will give me such a love?"

"I."

There was a moment of silence. Meera blushed and smiled. She let go of John's hand and went into a corner. John too smiled and thought of how he nearly expressed his affection for Meera. He was shy to express his feelings. But somehow what he did was enough an expression.

Roma on the other hand was thinking of this unusual occurrence. Whatever doubts Meera had were normal, but Roma had a different kind of perplexity. If this killer killed Nelmon then for what reason? Was it that Nelmon had seen him do something or was it something like revenge?

She walked to HN and looked at him.

"Are you lying HN?" she said.

"About Nelmon's death."

"No. All I said was that I experienced. And if you have any doubts then please confirm them."

HN's tone was a serious one. It looked as if he was very much serious about what he said.

"I didn't mean to hurt you but I think of being polite. I say you should be in police custody right now," Roma said.

"Fine," HN held his hands towards Roma.

"Don't try to melt her heart, HN." John came and gave a serious expression.

"I'm not," HN said.

"Really? Then why are you ready to come under police custody when you know you've done nothing." John said.

"I tried to prove I've not," HN said.

"You're a liar! Hironaga Maaki, son of Hibiki Maaki," John said furiously.

"I'm not lying! Doesn't matter what you think! I've done nothing," HN shouted back.

"Yes, Mr. Crimeproof. No one does anything, virtually but has to have done something practically," John yelled back.

This battle of words was growing heavy and Roma didn't know what to do.

She quickly went to bring Meera.

"I expect you to remain away from Roma. Dare if you get close to her!" John warned.

"Why does it even bother you my friendship with her?" HN said.

"Because I hate you and don't believe you!"

"You're just jealous!"

"I'm not. I know you killed Nelmon. I know you killed Mrs. Debbie and Roma's uncle! I know and I believe you're PSYCHO!"

Roma stood behind in surprise.

"Don't call him Psycho!" she yelled.

John soon was back to his senses and realized what he said. He, unspoken of a word, went away and Meera followed. HN went away without talking to Roma.

She was left alone with not a single soul to hold her. It all looked like a nightmare. She couldn't forget about it.

She reached back home with a blue face of sadness and a broken heart. Tee came to her and asked.

"What's wrong?"

"Nothing," Roma said and went to her room. Directly.

"Ok," Tee didn't bother her much because she knew when Roma was upset, she wouldn't like any interference.

But being a sister she had to know what was wrong with her.

Roma called HN but he didn't pick up. She knew he was not in a good mood because of what had happened. She tried a dozen times but no response.

"I don't know why I said such a nothing," she thought.

After some time, HN called back.

"I'm sorry!" Roma said.

"I do not want your apology because when you love someone you forgive them without the apology."

There was a pause from both sides for a moment.

"I love you! HN said.

"What do you mean?"

"I'm your friend. So I'm supposed to love you."

"Yes, I'm sorry. I didn't get it exactly."

"No problem. What did you think when I left?"

"I thought you were angry with me, so much that you didn't want to talk to me."

"I was but then I thought we're friends and it wasn't needed that I will be angry with you.

"You're nice. A very great friend. A very great?"

Roma burst into tears.

"What's wrong?"

"No.........no..............Nothing." Roma hung up and in a moment. HN stood in front of her. He wiped her tears and hugged her.

"I wanted a friend and I never hoped to have one. But once I met you, I felt I need to hope even though there is no option for me." Roma said.

"I promise you no matter what be the situation. I'm your only hope."

"Don't betray me! Ever!"

HN usually wasn't an emotional pal but today his eyes couldn't hold more. He also burst into tears.

"I won't. But you too don't. Please," He said.

What a friendship! Nevertheless, HN was Psycho no one could change the fact. No one even Roma or their friendship.

The next morning, when Roma reached the college, she found the whole college was decorated with flowers. And on a large banner on the front read, 'WELCOME! STAR OF OUR CAMPUS'

HN came to her and said, "They're happy for your hard work. What you did in India as a reporter."

"That's great or did you force them to do so," Roma said.

"What if I did? Doesn't matter."

"Ok."

Both went in and to the class.

Back at the office, John was reading some files of the incidents passed by. He was fed up with this dead-end he came upon every time. This was frustrating. But he found that this time it wasn't a dead-end actually, it was a tunnel.

A news report had enunciated an eyewitness who said that he had seen a person with a red-eye in an asylum. He had escaped the day the patients were being shifted.

He was a psychic person. He usually did not respond to any of the doctors who talked or treated him. He had lost his family in an accident.

When John had completed reading he smiled and called Meera the very moment.

When Meera got to know this discovery she was happy too.

"Looks like we are ready to catch the culprit," Meera said.

"No, not yet!" John said.

"Why?"

"It's not enough to prove the actual identity of Psycho."

"Ok. But we need to work on it. Promise?"

"Promise! Never actually want to break it."

"Alright. I'll go for now but I'm coming." John smiled and bid goodbye to Meera.

He then decided to do some research on his own. He went to HN's house. Like an exculpated burglar. John made his way into HN's home. The house was well maintained. The couch was carmine in color. The pillows set up on it were scarlet. The curtains had a violaceous appearance. There was a large rectangular table in front of the couch. A table in brown stood in the left corner of the room near the window. The window was small with a glass door about a meter away from it. Then on the right side of the hall was a small cabin and the door was small. It appeared wooden. Then a straight corridor is divided into a bedroom and kitchen. The house didn't have many accessories. Except for some pictures and paintings and magazines. A bookshelf stood beside the main door. John first searched the hall and the cabin. The only thing he found was some books related to law and judiciary.

So, for John searching the hall turned out to be un-purposeful. He then entered the bedroom. The bedroom had a large bed in the center with a large window behind it. To the left was the washroom and HN's wardrobe. The bed was covered in a bisque sheet with yellow pillows. The room too didn't have many bells and whistles. But the whole room was very well maintained and clean. In the room to there was a table and a bookshelf.

"I think he likes reading," John spoke to himself.

Now John searched the room but came to naught. Nothing as a clue showed up. John searched everywhere from the kitchen to the storeroom. At last, with nothing but impasse, John turned back to his house. This loss wasn't good at all but a waste of time. Suddenly John remembered that Meera was coming to meet him and he wasn't ready at all. What a job to be done!

He quickly changed his clothes and set up the table for dinner. Meera was due in time. John took a deep breath and brought her to the dining table.

"Nice. What for anyway?" Meera asked.

"Just to make our discussion comfortable," John answered.

"So what did you get in addition?"

"Nothing but that HN likes reading."

"Ok. But that isn't what we want."

"I know. He has left no clue. Very smart."

"So our prey is not a simple one but an astute one."

"Yes. It won't be easy to catch him. Though," John got up and brought two filled glasses.

"I don't know how long I can last without Nelmon," he sighed.

It was nearly tea-time when HN reached and found something wrong with his house. He looked carefully and noticed that his things were displaced from their position.

"Someone has been here," he said.

But he didn't mind it because neither anything was taken nor disturbed. He laughed to himself.

"Oh, dear. John! You're still not on the tip of the iceberg. Where I am patiently waiting for you."

Soon it was dusk and HN sat for dinner. Suddenly someone knocked at the door.

"Who may I be expecting now?" HN asked.

"John Woven, UNSC detective," John said.

HN opened the door and as soon as he did John hit his head so hard that he fell and blacked out.

The moment HN opened his eyes he found himself in a small dark barely lit cabin with a table in front of him. At first, he could not see who was standing in front of him but soon he recognized it was John.

"What do you need?" he asked.

"Can I ask you a few things?" John catechized.

"Like what?"

"Are you Psycho?"

"Nice. No!"

"How many people have you killed?"

"None!"

"Stop lying," John slapped the table hard and said with a wrathful voice.

"I'm not lying," said HN.

"You're!"

"What makes you think that I'm just not saying the truth?"

"Well, well, look after doing a little bit of research we find that the day Psycho, or you to mention, escaped from the asylum four officers died unusually. Their death was similar to that of the person who attacked you in the hospital."

"He died because he fell off the building."

"No, he died when he fell off the building."

HN gave a villainy smile and brought John closer to him.

"I'm PSYCO! No matter what you do, you won't be able to get me until and unless I want you to."

HN pushed John and said, "So, now what do you want?"

John had to say nothing. It seemed awkward for a criminal to so easily challenge justice. Though he got to know that HN was Psycho, how would he ever make the world believe who he is?

John came out of the cabin and went out.

Looking around he thought, “What is the world even thinking about Psycho?”

The world believed that Psycho was the only justice in the world on whom they could count on!

9

BEWITCHMENT OF JUSTICE

NPA, Japan, Tokyo, Chiyoda:

The police were having a meeting about some international affairs. The Director-General of NPA, Mitsushiro Suzuki, grabbed onto one of the files kept in from of him and said, "The only international affair no one has taken care of lies in my hands now."

"What, sir?" asked Hiromi(Kaya).

"On the eve of Christmas, a young boy's father and mother died in a car accident. This young boy was taken into an asylum and kept there for nearly 4 or 5 years. This boys' name is Hironaga Maaki. Our mission is to bring him back to Japan. He may decide his nationality himself."

So on the order of the Director-General of NPA, a term of four Japanese officials were sent to find HN.

Coming back to our base in America, when John got this news he quickly informed Meera.

"What's so important in this?" she asked.

"If they take HN, to be precise Psycho, then his base will be changed. We won't be able to capture him. I suppose one of the team members is Hiromi. It'd be better if you inform her and say about this," John replied.

"Fine, as you say."

Meera knew John's zephyr-like concern. He knew that even though HN would be taken to Japan the process of capturing him won't change. Still, he wanted this all to be done at his previous base. This seemed easier. She, therefore, called Hiromi and told her everything she could. Hiromi got the idea and, being the head of the team, changed plans.

"We're now going to help FBI arrest HN!"

But the enemy was not a single step behind the police. He had an intelligent devil, mind. HN knew that NPA had sent a team of officials to capture him. To keep his work untouched and to keep the police headless about it, he planned a big trap for the FBI and NPA. The G-7 summit in Washington D.C! where Psycho's targets are all together!

Preparations were being made for the G-7 summit which was to be held in Breton Woods, New Hampshire, Mount Washington Hotel. Build in the nineties was situated near Mount Washington. A vast green land lay upon its feet with the mountain situated behind it. The FBI and some government officials came to welcome the Finance Ministers of France, Italy, Germany, Japan, the UK, and Canada. HN followed all the events and waited patiently for his move.

John feared whether something would go wrong. So he kept a close look on the security of the officials of the countries. Nothing was supposed to go wrong but something did. What? Let's see.

The officials from different countries sat for the meeting. It was the first day of the summit and Psycho had put a surprise for them.

The meeting went smoothly until the lunch arrived. Everyone was having a pleasureful lunch. The silence and calmness were warning but none understand it. Suddenly the Japanese finance minister was shot and he fell. This created panic and everyone ran here and there. All of sudden two simultaneous blasts took place and the officers quickly evacuated everyone.

The ambulances came and the injured were shifted to the hospitals. The dead, whoever found, were brought out while some of them were under the debris.

John couldn't understand how this happened. Even after so much security how did the bombs and the shooter enter the hotel. It was very confusing.

The news of the attack spread quickly and people started expressing worry about the attack.

John sat in the office listening to the news.

"A sudden attack at Mount Washington Hotel, in Breton Woods has claimed 14 lives. There was a simultaneous shooting and blast in the Hotel. Japanese Finance Minister Kono Aibiki also is among the dead. The police are still following the tracks."

John had this in mind that the actual person behind everything which had happened was Psycho. However, he didn't want to tell about this to anyone, still though John couldn't figure how did the weapon get a chance of being used. His thought was disturbed by a call. A call from Psycho.

"I know what you're thinking right now," he said.

"You think you're very intelligent. I suppose you're the biggest fool on the Earth," John replied.

"Aw! You're so, so, so, innocent, Psycho replied.

"I'm not!"

"Ok, let me explain what has happened: What mistake did you do?"

A day ago…

When HN pulled John closer to him to tell him that he was the Psycho they were looking for, he put a small device on John. It'd let him know everything.

"So now what do you want," HN said.

John left helpless and tired. He reached home and got a call that the NPA had sent four officials to get HN. That's where HN got to know about this news, of both the NPA and G-7 summit.

The next step was to get the bombs and gun into the hotel, pass the security. It was done by putting bombs in the regular food supply of the hotel. The one who received it was under Psycho's control. He took the bombs into the kitchen and hid them. Next came the gun. It was very easy. Psycho got one of the security guards under control and got his work done. Easier than he thought!

John stood in wonder and amazement. What in the world was HN? A human or a superhuman?

How could John not consider even the little bit of the thing?

"Look John there can be two things: either I'm very intelligent or you're very much a fool!" and Psycho hung up.

John threw the phone on the floor violently and kicked the table hard.

"I'm a fool!"

On hearing the sound of something breaking, Meera came up to see. She found John crying badly.

"What happened?" she asked.

"I've lost! I've lost to Psycho!"

The NPA had reached America on the second day of the summit. They, without wasting a second, went to the FBI headquarters. John and Meera were not there. It was only Roma but Hiromi was told by Meera not to say anything.

"We're here for some official work. Could we meet Mr. John and Ms. Meera?" Hiromi asked.

"They are not here right now. Have a seat. I'll call them," Roma said.

She called John and Meera immediately.

The NPA and the FBI sat for a meeting.

"Look, we believe HN Maaki, a Japanese- American, is Psycho. We need to capture him as soon as possible before he ruins the whole world!" John said.

Meera looked at him and smiled. She had given this pal a long sermon of braveness, only then did he get back to his senses.

The NPA agreed to all terms and conditions.

"Let's see what the future holds for us!" John said.

Psycho versus John, who's going to win?

A happy and healthy morning welcomed everyone to start a new day with new hope, especially for John, who nearly had lost hope the previous day.

Roma also got up thinking to forget about whatever had happened the previous days. From her uncle's to Mrs. Debbie's death. A report on several criminals in the US reached John. He found a drastic decrease in the number of criminals all over America. Though the criminal activities had increased, all accounting to Psycho.

"Nice, but not very much healthy nice," John said.

He reached the office early and waited for others to come. The first to arrive after John was an NPA officer Kishiro Musai.

"Good morning!" John said with a healthy tone.

"Good morning," Kishiro greeted.

"How do they say in your country?"

"Ohaiyo Goazimasu!"

"They'll be coming soon!"

Kishiro sat near John and sighed.

"Something wrong?"

"Kind of. I saw an unusual-looking person. He followed me till here. I sighed because he's gone now."

"Ok." John at once could guess who he could be Psycho.

Meera also arrived by them.

"I've got the news. The US Secretary was on a two-day visit to Afghanistan. He's returning by tonight. He wants tight security to be held," she said.

"Fine! I'm going to work on this now!" John, to save the Secretary, went into his office to arrange security. But would be able to save the US Secretary or not was a big question

John looked over the security set up again and again. Then he thought something. It was better, he didn't let the people know that the Secretary was coming.

"Look Meera, let me appoint the driver for the Secretary. His identity should be kept a secret," John said.

Meera agreed. She believed in every step John took.

The driver, Josh, was appointed to pick up the Secretary around 09:00 pm, except for John, no one else knew who Josh was. The driver arrived to pick up the Secretary. It was raining heavily. The Secretary reached his house and his assistant came to welcome him, only to find his Sir dead on the floor. He quickly called John.

When John reached there, he asked the assistant to tell him everything.

"I heard the sound of the horn, so I came down to receive him and when I reached down de way lying on the floor like that," the assistant said.

"Where is the driver?" asked John.

The very moment Josh entered in and said, "Sir, I'm here. Shall I leave to pick the Secretary?"

"What?! The time was 09:00 P.M, not half-past nine!" John yelled.

"But I got a message from Ms. Roma that time was half-past nine!" Josh said.

"Roma!" John was stunned.

"She'd never do that!" Meera, who also was accompanying John said.

"I'm sorry. But I'm telling the truth. If you want to see, you can see the message," Josh showed them the message he had got from Roma's number.

There was no way John could deny it. It was Roma's number for sure. Roma was summoned there.

"Why did you message Josh the wrong time of pick up?" John asked.

"I didn't message anything at all!" Roma said.

"But what's this then?" John said.

Roma looked at the number from which the message came she was shocked.

"I didn't. Look, you can look at my phone!"

Roma held her phone to John and he looked. In the previous records, he found a message sent to Josh.

"You are lying Roma!" John burst out with a loud voice.

"No, I'm not! Believe me!"

Roma cried and went away. Meera followed her up to her car.

"Roma listen! I believe you. John will too," she said.

"No, she won't! he won' at all!" Roma cried.

"He will come," Meera held Roma's hand and took her to John.

He hugged Roma and said, "I didn't mean to hurt you. I'm sorry. I know you haven't done anything. I believe."

Roma smiled and said, "I think Psycho did it, what say?"

"You're right. He is way too intelligent than we think," John said.

They took Josh with them to ensure he remained safe. They had to do something to keep the death of the Secretary a secret. Otherwise, it'd spread a bad message and many pro-government people might blame the opposition.

"Now what do we do?" said Meera.

"Let's do this. I'll say you message the CNN news channel to put this headline," John said pointing towards Roma.

Roma called the news channel head and told them that a report had come that the US Secretary had a sudden heart stroke and passed away. The head of the CNN network, Carlson Bose, who loved Roma like his own daughter, believed her, and soon on the Prime Time CNN news, the headline was reported. This seemed a little odd for the people but that was a lie colored in truth which everyone was supposed to believe. John or Roma probably couldn't reveal their carelessness or say Psycho's intelligence. It'd mislead the people. That is not what John wanted.

But it was too late for John. People had already taken to Psycho's path. They had started believing him blindly. Even those who were the pillars of justice. When justice is working for crime then what is justice? A supporter or oppose of truth? Psycho had already, stealthily, bewitched the justice of the world.

"I'm the future of justice. Justice is the new God of this world! Behold! Don't try to escape. You will be dead before you even know you are ...." Psycho

After the headline, there was a live voice. It was, obviously, Psycho's voice. He told the people that the news was a lie. That the secretary had died because he had robbed the people of their opportunities and dreams. Soon after he addressed the people, a protest broke out near the FBI office.

"What's this! How can they believe Psycho!" Roma said.

"He is misleading them and that's not right!" Meera said.

We can do nothing about it. It'd seem odd for me to say such a thing but Psycho, nevertheless, is right in his opinion. These corrupt and rich people, criminals also, are just ruining the world. Despite that, they still need to have a right to live. A petty thief should not deserve death while a murdered who has brutally killed someone deserves it. Psycho, even so, is treating them all the same," John said.

"I think you're right. We are helpless, after all, if our public isn't supporting us," Roma said.

The protest continued till evening and then on people started dispersing. The sun had nearly been lost and the moon was about to take charge of the time thereafter.

John gazed at the fading sunlight. The lights in the city started turning up one by one until the whole city appeared like a world of stars. That was the spirit of America. John never wanted to be done for. The busy streets, glittering shops and houses, the people walking by and the tall and alpine buildings were the beauty of the city. None less. It was the victim of Psycho's solicitude regards criminals.

"I swear by the life of those people you killed that even if takes my whole life I will wipe out you of this world. Psycho!" said John.

He held on to his coat and left for home. He reached there and called Meera to come and meet him. She reached his house quickly and came in.

"Everything of, John?" she asked.

"Yeah! Fine, everything's fine!" John replied.

"They why did you call me?"

"I had to say something to you."

"Please!"

John held Meera's hands and said, "Will you marry me?"

Meera smiled and looked down. John could smell his answer and said, "It's a yes. Right?"

Meera nodded.

"It's a yes!"

John was so happy that he jumped in joy and yelled at top of his voice, "I'm happy!"

"John! Stop it. Nonsense" Meera said.

"Sorry about that but I'm just too excited and happy," said John.

On spur of the moment, the bell rang. John opened the door and found a man washed in his sweat. His cheek was a little pudgy and eyebrows nearly consolidated with hair. He had a thin layer of hair around his face, his clothes shabby, and his body meagre in comparison to his cheeks.

"Well, who are you?" John asked.

"Bosh Ray. Former FBI officer," the man replied.

John was shocked. The man's appearance didn't prove to help to know his identity.

"Mr. Ray. I think I know you. You were the one who was given the case of the Bulgaria ship attack" John said.

"Right," Mr. Ray said.

"Please come in."

John brought him in and gave him water.

"A long story of how I reached here," Mr. Ray said.

"No worries. You take care time," John said.

"As you know I've retired and that when I was of your age I used to be very popular. But, a question might arise in your mind, how am I meeting you in this disfigured appearance. Well after my retirement I fell into large debt of some one million dollars due to some reason. I had to sell everything and so I was left with nothing but these clothes and my old soul. Recently I heard the news of someone called Psycho killing corrupt people. I don't support him although I expect him to kill someone who put me under this debt. His name is Alan Son. He and I used to be very good friends but he started being jealous of my popularity. I went to some people asking about someone who could help me. A person, someone, I don't know and he put on unusual clothing, told me about you," Mr. Ray said.

"Could you tell me his clothing more precisely?"

"He was wearing a cap. Over which he wore the hood of his jacket and he also wore a mask. His left eye was hidden by his hair."

"Do you know you've met this popular killer himself?"

"What! You mean the person who told me about you was Psycho!"

"Yes, sir."

"My goodness! Why'd he by the way lead me to you?"

"That's what I'm thinking. Unusual but dangerous!"

Mr. Ray got up and ran his hands around his back. John looked around to see at the clock the time and on his turning back he saw a gun pointed towards him. The gunman Mr. Ray.

Before he could respond, Mr. Ray shot him and he fell. The perpetrator left the scene immediately. Meera was in the washroom and she quickly came to see what happened. She found her husband-to-be lying on the floor with a gunshot on his chest. "John!" she screamed. Meera was shocked as if the whole world had crumbled down in front of her. She had planned so much of the future with him and imagined so many good things together but it was all taken away in seconds. She was helpless and couldn't think of anything. The neighbours heard the gunshot and came in for help. They called the ambulance and also the police.

The ambulance was there in no time and John was taken to the hospital. Roma also came there to help and comfort Meera.

"What exactly happened?" she asked.

"I don't get it. Someone had come to meet him. After the man came in, I went to the washroom. Then I heard a gunshot and came out to see him shot down. I think the man shot at him. He called himself Mr. Bosh Ray," Meera said.

"Don't worry everything will be alright," Roma said.

The treatment was underway but the doctor hadn't given any information about John's health.

Meera was worried sick about John. She knew if something happened to him then no one could stop Psycho. The whole night went worrying for the girls. Until in the morning, the doctor came and told Meera that it was lucky that John survived a death trap but he might remain unconscious for some time.

"At least he's alive," Meera said with tears in her eyes.

Roma held her and hugged her.

"Don't worry. Just to say I am going to the college so I'm going to keep HN here," she said.

"I don't think I need him. I'm happy without him," Meera said.

"Why?"

"Is he not supposed to go to college?"

"Yes, but he can skip a day if I say that he's needed."

"No, thanks."

Meera forced Roma out of the room before she could say something. But still, Roma sent HN to be with Meera. She wasn't happy at all.

"So who tried to kill John?" HN asked.

"None of your business!" Meera responded but with a slow voice.

"Sorry?"

"Nothing. Let's not talk about what happened."

"Fine."

There was nothing that Meera and HN would talk about so there was silence in the room. After some hours of quiescent expression, HN got up and ordered some tea. HN knew what thought Meera was having.

"Did John tell you about me?" he asked.

"What?" Meera said.

"Ok, he didn't," HN said.

"Look, doesn't matter whether he said what he had to or not. The thing is that at least we think you're Psycho!"

"Oh! That's the thing. Well, let me tell you my little secret. I am Psycho!"

Meera stood in an utter jolt. She didn't know what to do. She was face-to-face with Psycho, the world's biggest enemy.

"Don't worry, but, I won't kill you!" Psycho said.

"You say so but I don't believe you!" Meera went outside.

HN stood inside. He looked around and then outside. Every person had someone with whom he or she could share pains but not Psycho, He was a loner. He had no one.

"Why me? Why?" he said.

Meera had a severe conflict in her mind, whether she should tell Roma HN was Psycho or not.

She waited long hours for Roma to come. She didn't want to remain with HN anymore. But Roma didn't arrive. She called her and Roma said that she had some important work to do so she will be late to arrive.

It was around dinner time. HN had his dinner and was waiting for Meera.

"Didn't you've dinner?" he asked.

"I'll order myself. Not to mention that you could mix poison with it," she said.

"Seriously? You think I'm like a villain of any drama," HN said.

"I wish you were," Meera said.

They were talking when the lights went off suddenly.

"Don't say it's your plan Psycho," Meera said.

"No, not mine at least," HN replied.

"Then must be some normal power cut."

"That's lucid."

"Let's wait. Just don't kill me or something. Whatever you do?"

"Why would kill you! I have better things to do, like trying to find my phone for torchlight or a candle maybe."

"Just do something!"

The light, however, didn't come for a while. And soon HN and Meera heard someone lock a door, they fear it was theirs. HN checked and found that it was indeed their door that was locked from outside. Meera started to panic.

"Don't say we're stuck together for eternity!" Meera said.

"Looks like we're!" HN replied.

"No way I'm staying with you here," Meera said

The two slowly headed towards the window of the room to call for help. The whole city was covered in darkness, not a single building or house was lit with light. Something was wrong with the power supply of the city. Even after so many calls of help, none come for succor.

"What's wrong with everyone? No one is coming for help," Meera said.

"My phone's dead," HN said.

"Great! Useful for crime and useless when saving someone."

"It's a phone. Does not work on someone's say? When the battery is dead it's dead. Nothing we can do."

"Really?"

"By the way, my phone has been used for the torchlight for the previous 45 minutes. Got it?"

Suddenly they heard someone open the door. A torch beam fell on HN's face and a voice said.

"HN? Is that you?"

"Yes, and may I know who you are?" HN said.

"John!" Meera exclaimed.

"What?" HN said…

"Yes, it's me. Unusual to know but it's true," John said.

He led the two out and into his hospital room.

"The doctor said," Meera was saying and John interrupted.

"I know. Look, I opened my eyes and heard your voice. So I got off my bed and with the torch came to find you."

"You shouldn't have. You need rest."

HN looked at the two and said, "Can I leave?"

"No," John replied.

"It'd be better if he would," Meera said.

"No, I have to talk to him, in privacy," John said.

"Ok, but just to say, be careful," Meera left the room to the two of them.

"So what do you need?" HN started the conversation.

"You sent Mr. Ray, didn't you?" asked John.

"Let's see. He said that a guy just looking like Psycho told him your address and then he tried to kill you. Yes! I sent him! HN replied."

"Why do you want to kill me? Because you fear I'll reveal your truth to Roma!"

"No! I don't fear you! I just want my work to be smooth without any hurdle."

"Wrong! You don't want Roma to know who you're which she probably will get to know from me."

"Yes, I don't. Fine?"

"Why? You can let me know. You can let Nelmon know and someone else, why not Roma?'

"Because I don't!"

"Why?!"

HN closed his eyes and a drop of tear fell down his cheek. He sat down and took a deep breath.

"If there is anyone in this whole world whom I think I can share anything with, she's Roma. After so many years. I've felt secure with someone."

"Is there something you want to share?" John asked.

"I was tortured!" HN cried, woefully and with short breaths.

"Who tortured you?"

"This world! Every person whom I met! After I lost my parents I was forcibly taken into the asylum and was declared mad. I wasn't. I was just scared and felt lonely. But when they put me in with mad people around, I started feeling frustrated and became mad!"

"You can give yourself a chance, A chance to be a normal person. Maybe like Roma."

"I'm not changing myself just because I fear Roma will hate me for who I am!" HN said.

"You're stubborn!" John said.

"If you can, then try to figure out my intelligence."

HN went out and said to Meera, "Go in! your soon-to-be husband is waiting for you!"

He went out in the dark streets of D.C, with nothing but moonlight.

Meera came in and asked John about his collogues with HM.

"Didn't turn out well for me. All I got to know is that he isn't mad. He was forced to be one," John replied.

"Look, I know you'll be feeling for him right now. But if he isn't ready to change, you cannot do anything," Meera said.

"You're right. Looks like I gotta do it the thick-skinned hardcore way."

An unusual typical morning lay in wait for John and his team. John woke up and still leaving his dreams was freaked out by Meera.

"Ah! Quit it! You gave me a heart attack!" he said.

"I'm sorry. But I gotta bad news." Meera replied.

"Doctors say if starting a day with the news. It should be good. Bad ones are usually a menace to health."

"It's not time for Jokes. Be serious!"

"Proceed."

"Come out and see for yourself what bad news is awaiting you."

As soon as John stepped out, he was welcomed by a protest. Not that it was on one idea. People supporting Psycho, and those who didn't, both the groups were having a share on roads.

"It happened yesterday too. It will fade," John said.

"No, it won't. It's worldwide," Meera said.

"Couldn't you give me good news like Psycho suicided or he surrendered," John said?

"How about this? They're selling Pro-Psycho tablets for 5$," Meera said.

"Really?!"

"No!"

Roma somehow found her way through the mad crowd into the office.

"I dropped my burger. We've got billions of Psycho's to handle," she said.

She was right. Even the Anti-Psycho protesters were acting like maniacs. They were like Pro-Psycho physically but Anti-Psycho mentally.

"Turn on the TV. Gotta have a look at the rest of this vale," John said.

The group tuned in to the news to check for updates around the world. So Meera held right about the protest around the world. Not only the USA, but Japan, China, India, South Korea, Russia, the whole of Europe, and a few African countries were protesting. At some places, people had broken into government offices and had enkindled all the files. In an hour or so reports of death started smashing in from around the world. But the people repudiated and brushed off all the warnings.

"I hope it will ebb by evening," Roma said.

"But what about until then?" John said.

"He's right. Already fifteen unfortunate deaths have been reported across 61 countries. And who knows how many more countries will join and how many more will die," Meera said.

"It's still 9 am. We've got, who knows, how many of unpropitious hours till this nonsense dies down," John said.

"Just trying to comfort, to keep up our hopes," Roma said as her smile for sanguineness decolorized.

The group sat down with no idea what to do while Psycho had his every step completely planned. He knew that the FBI couldn't possibly kill people for two reasons. One, John wouldn't let them and second, it will create a bad image in front of the public. We all know protesting is a right & the FBI was helpless in front of that. But it wasn't a peaceful protest too. So, the FBI wasn't tied totally. They could arrest the organizers of the protesters. Nonetheless, Psycho uses it to bring more people on his side. FBI's bête noire wasn't easy to defeat.

John couldn't, however, take more of it. He had to somehow put an end to this protest.

"I have an idea. But it's only a theoretical one. If only somehow we could bring Psycho to stop these protests," John said.

"How?" asked Meera.

"That's what's causing the problem. At this point of time the people, especially the Pro's, will only respond to Psycho's call," John replied.

"I know how we can get it practical," Roma added her part.

"Wherewith?" Meera asked.

"If our Psycho's ready to go out," Roma replied.

Both John and Meera starred at the young mind in utter amazement. John got her message. Someone had to act Psycho in front of the people because the people didn't know him so it'd be easy to feel them with a fake one. And the one to act it out would be our John.

By lunch, the protest grew larger and many more countries joined in. So far Roma was wrong about the protest fading. But she at least had a plan to fade it. John was getting ready to act on Psycho, and Meera and Roma were setting the stage.

"What if Psycho, during my act, confirms that I'm not him?" John asked.

"Don't worry, I've got this under control," Roma said.

"I hope so."

In a moment of time FBI's Psycho was ready to fool the people. His speech was to be aired on almost every channel, starting from CNN.

The airing started at around 1:30 P.M. But before John could start, the actual Psycho took over.

"I respect the way you are protesting, using your right, and fighting for them. But you're doing it with violence. I, my people, want it peaceful. You're letting live on stake. Don't do this. I want an end to this violence. I hope you don't let me down.

And a message to my beloved inquisitor. Nice try being me! He said.

The airing stopped and the people went to a whist atmosphere of protest.

"Why'd he do this?" John said.

"Maybe he doesn't want violence," Roma said.

"Something's wrong. He could've done it a long time ago. But he choose to only when we were to," Meera said.

"That's what I'm thinking. And how did he know that we were about to air on TV," John said.

Someone knocked at the door and said, "A recorded tape for Mr. Waven."

"That'd be me," John came out to take it. Wasting no time he opened it and listened.

"John, my dear nemesis, I'm sorry you didn't get to air on TV but someday you'll. Maybe when you'll say that you won't try to catch me anymore. I like to explain to you how I was able to fool you. But I won't do it this time. If you can, guess it on your own," and it stopped.

John stood staring at the recorded tape with nothing to say. He took a deep breath and smoke.

"Roma, I'd want you to leave me and Meera in privacy for some time."

"Ok," confused, Roma went out.

John looked at Meera and said,

"I don't know how, but HN did put some bug here in this room. What did he say about the power cut yesterday?"

"He said he wasn't involved in it. I just don't believe it. But I don't see what motive he might have had behind the power cut," Meera replied.

"We discussed the plan in another room, not in either of the rooms where he was."

"So? I don't get your point?"

"I'll explain. The power cut meant that the cameras wouldn't have worked. Let's say a group of people come and fix bugs in every corner of the hospital. They also hack into the security system so they can see the footage from the camera at the hospital."

"That's ok. But he could have mended with the power supply of the hospital only."

"He didn't because it'd have caused attention. When the whole city was on blackout, it seemed a normal power cut."

"I, see!"

"However, I am still not able to gather up why he chose to speak to the protesters?"

"Whatever the case be, he's up to something."

So the protest was peaceful and no causality was reported thereafter. The protests were so damn serious about protesting that nobody, not a single soul, left the sight of protest.

Roma sat outside in the cold fluttering wave, looking at what one of the most talked-about countries had turned into. The silence of, once the busy streets pricked her. She couldn't bear what Psycho had done to her country. She looked at the buildings when she saw a shadow approaching her. So dark was the atmosphere that nothing could be seen of the umbrage.

"Who, may I ask, are you?"

The figure came closer to Roma and crooked towards her car.

"Psycho," he said in a slow and quiet voice.

Before Roma could scream for help. He put his hands on her mouth.

"Let's take you on a tour!" He said and quickly gave her a knockout.

Back at the hospital, John & Meera were discussing Psycho's further plans, unaware of the episode that took place.

"I think we should send Roma back home," John said.

"Ok, I'll go to her."

Meera came down to talk to Roma only to find that she wasn't there. John also came down.

"She might have gone home," John said.

"No. Her sister send me to bring her," HN came from behind.

"What do you mean by that?" John asked.

"If she's not here or in her house, the where's she?" HN questioned back.

"I don't know," John said

"How could you be so careless!" HN slammed.

"Ok, I accept I was careless! Now tell us where you've kept her Psycho!" John said.

"Psycho? What the heck are you talking about? I'm HN, not Psycho!"

John looked at him surprised with nothing to utter. Meera too was taken aback but she countered it.

"Now, what dirty trick are you up to?" she said.

"Are you people out of your mind! I get it Psycho might've kidnapped Roma but you calling me Psycho makes no sense!" HN said.

"Stop lying!" John said.

"Well then, if I were Psycho why on earth would I kidnap Roma! Answers it!" HN hit the iron. Neither John nor Meera could counter it. They went silent.

"Answer! Why are not you answering!" HN said.

"Because we don't have one," John said accepting that he had lost.

"So, I want Roma safely and soundly back. Otherwise, I don't know what'll do to that Psycho!" HN left angry.

John stood with two things to solve in his mind. Firstly, why did HN deny being Psycho although he had accepted being him a long time ago? Secondly, if Psycho had kidnapped Roma how could John possibly save her?

Roma sat in a corner of a small room with walls of stone and a small window with a dwarf door by its side. Her mouth was tied and so were her hands.

"Hmm…….!" She tried to call out for help but it was pointless. There was no one except for a small mouse searching for something to nibble in the room. Soon Roma heard someone unlock the door.

"Roma, right?" the man said. He was a man in his thirties with a bit of a rather stylish dark irony black beard and a very much bright face. He was wearing a cap in a red and black brown outfit.

"Hmm!" Roma replied. That was, after all, what she could say.

"Good! Here's your pizza," the man kept a box of pizza with a drink beside her and then untied her. He went out and looked at the door.

Although Roma was hungry she didn't touch anything. After some time somebody again unlocked the door and this time it was Psycho.

"Well, look at you, I'm not hungry at all, are you?" he said.

"I am! But I'm not eating anything!" Roma sid.

"Any cause? Would like to hear if it's special," he said.

Roma didn't say anything further. But she couldn't keep quiet for a much longer time, so she asked.

"Why did you kidnap me? All I know is you didn't do it to kill me because I don't know who you're."

"Yes, nice question. I did it for I'm planning a very big thing and I want you to go and tell John that the life of the chief of UNSC is in danger. Come, I may take you around my small place."

"Couldn't you send a message, as you usually do?"

"I was bored of it. That's why."

"I'm not coming with you anywhere!" Roma said.

"Either you come or," Psycho showed Roma a picture of HN and continued, "or he dies!"

Roma couldn't say anything. She didn't want to risk HN's life. So she agreed to go with him. Psycho took her around his small house made of stones. It was cold in there. There was no light, no big windows or accessories'. It was a damp-looking place with only one room of much interest. It was a room with computers everywhere.

"My base, it is," Psycho said.

"Why are you revealing everything to me? May I ask?" Roma asked.

"Don't worry. You won't remember a bit of it after you leave."

Roma didn't get it but she knew Psycho's intentions weren't very welcoming.

After giving her a tour around, Psycho prepared to bid goodbye to Roma.

"But keep in mind don't to say anything to HN or he will see the last of this world," he said.

"I get it. Now leave me."

Roma was taken in a black car to the Capital One Arena which, already mentioned, isn't for from the FBI headquarters. After dropping Roma there, the car left. She looked around and there was no one until she saw a tall figure approach her. It was HN.

"HN!" Roma ran to him and hugged him. But soon stepped back.

"How did you know I was here?" she asked.

"Somebody, most probably Psycho, called me to come and pick you up in the Arena," HN replied.

"Oh!" Roma held his hand and quickly darted to the exit.

"I got news for you. The President of UNSC, who happens to be in America, was shot dead at his residence an hour ago," HN said.

"What!"

"Yes, but you look shocked as if you did expect it so soon!"

"Well, Psycho had told me to inform John that the President's life was in danger. But I didn't expect him to kill him already."

HN held her hand and smiled.

"You worry too much. Not good for your health at this age," he said.

"Thanks for your concern. But I've promised myself until I don't bring Psycho to justice I won't clam down for an instant," Roma said.

"Best of luck, hope you win."

"Let's go. I got to talk to John."

Both went to the office to meet John. He was worried about Roma. He saw her with HN, was happy but a little more worried because she was with HN.

"Roma, you're okay! I mean," John behaved shockingly and surprisingly.

"Yes, I am fine. But there's something I gotta tell you. Psycho told me to tell you that the life of the President of the UNSC is in danger. Looks like I was late," Roma said.

"Why'd he tell you something which he would do while you were in captive? Meera asked.

"I don't know! That's what is confusing!" Roma said.

"I think Roma needs to rest," HN interrupted the conversation.

Roma was about to deny but HN said, "who knows whether you've eaten something or not. You'll have something to eat and then you'll rest. Following this, you may want to talk."

Roma couldn't say no and went to eat something accompanied by Meera. John and HN were left in the same room looking at each other.

John was still confused about the denial from HN of being Psycho all of sudden. Was it that Psycho had framed HN? Or was it Psycho's yet another game to fool John? Whatever it was, it wasn't good at all. John had reached so close to Psycho's identity and now in a matter of time, he's back to where he started.

"Can I ask you something, John?" HN said.

"Yes, please," John replied.

"Maybe Psycho kidnapped Roma for something else."

"Like what?"

"I cannot say, I don't know. But just saying."

"You told me that you're Psycho. Do you remember?"

"No, I never said I'm Psycho. I'm not Psycho at all."

"What's going on?" why is this happening? Thought John.

John's phone rang the very moment. It was George Haselwood.

"Yeah, George," John answered.

"The NPA officials which had arrived here, we're living in at Hamilton Hotel, Right?" George asked.

"Yes, what happened?" John said.

"Four of them have disappeared!" George said.

"Psycho diverted me in saving Roma and! Oh, no!" a thought came into John's mind.

"I'll send their names," George hung up.

HN stood there looking at John's expression of worry and defeat.

"So, looks like you've lost to me, after all, John."

Accept your defeat!"

10

THE DENOUEMENT (FALL OF THE WORLD)

UNITED NATIONS SECURITY COUNCIL, MEETING SESSION, NEW YORK:

"How many of you have lost a family member to crime?"

Began the new President of UNSC, Ethan Alex, "Tell me! How many? Almost every one of us is fed up with the criminal world. We all want to get rid of this crime in our world. So, today we together will support each other to get rid of the crimes done around the world. We support Psycho!"

John hit the table hard and then threw the remote onto the wall.

"Ah! I'm fed up with him!" John kicked the wall and screamed out loudly again, doing it repeatedly.

Suddenly he saw Psycho standing in front of him, laughing.

"You coward!" John said.

But it disappeared. Meera came to him after hearing his scream.

"What's wrong?" She asked.

"I don't know! He was here a moment ago but then he was gone!" John said crying.

"Who was were?"

"Psycho! He was here right now! Look! Meera! He's there!"

Meera turned around but there was no one.

"There is no one, John!" she said.

"But he was there. How could you not see him!" John said.

Meera couldn't understand what was happening to John. Why was he acting so oddly?

Roma also entered the very moment.

"Meera, the Japanese Foreign Minister wants to talk to John," she said.

"John isn't okay right now!" Meera said.

"No, I'm fine!" John held himself and went down to talk to the Minister.

"Yes," he said.

The talk wasn't very long but short enough to push John's self-confidence even more down. Roma and Meera came in and said, "What did he say?"

"The Japanese have decided to break all the contacts with America, especially FBI, for their carelessness and irresponsibility regards the NPA officials who had come here," John replied.

"They can't do this! We need NPA to help us catch Psycho!" Meera said.

"They won't help, anymore. We have to do this on our own!" John said and went out.

"But," Meera couldn't figure what to say.

John came out to breathe a little although he couldn't feel the air around him. The world around him, he felt as if it didn't exist at all. A bloody ambience enclaved the world. Psycho had mutilated the world's life. And John had failed to save the realm.

"John!" Meera called out to him.

"What?" John answered.

"Look, I know you're a little off track, but you need to buckle up a little. We need you," Meera said.

"I'm fine!" John said.

"You're not! Do you know how you acted up in the room? You started having visions. You said you saw Psycho for a moment and then he disappeared. And you're saying you're fine!" Meera countered.

John burst into heavy tears and screamed out loudly. It appeared that he was in deep pain. Meera could see what had happened to John. He couldn't fight Psycho anywhere. He was tired of going around in circles, running after the same thing.

Roma came the very moment and saw how John had fallen on his knees and wasn't able to lift himself.

'What has happened to John? Why's he crying?' she thought.

HN followed Roma and as soon as John saw him, he got up and advanced towards him.

"You liar!" John held HN by his neck and started vilifying him.

HN played his defense and pushed John to the ground. He took a deep breath and coughed. John got hold of a stone and threw it at HN.

"Ah!" HN screamed.

"You are a cheater! A liar! A murderer!" John said.

"John! Stop it!" Roma said while handling HN who had his face washed in blood.

Meera held John back.

"Stop it, John? What're you doing?" she said.

"You know he's Psycho! Don't you, Meera!" John said whimpering.

"Psycho?" Roma said, "He's not!"

"Roma, take HN. He's bleeding, badly," Meera said.

Roma took HN but with a mind filled with questions.

'Why'd John call HN, Psycho?' she thought.

Meera brought John to her house and laid him down on the bed.

"You need to rest. I'll bring something to eat," Meera went down to the kitchen to cook something for John. But when she returned to the room, John wasn't there. The window of the room was open,

"John! Where did he go?" Meera panicked and quickly called Roma.

"I'm sorry to disturb but where are you?" Meera asked.

"In HN's home. Why?" Roma announced.

"Look for John, he could come there. I'll be coming soon."

Meera hung up and left for HN's house. Before she could reach, John had already tried to assail HN. Roma was trying to stop him. And when Meera arrived, a group of police officers was taking John.

"Wait!" Meera came to them.

"Meera, I'm sorry! I had to. He nearly killed HN," Roma said.

"But, you should have waited till I came!" Meera said when eyes caught the sight of HN being taken to hospital.

"See! Now you know. If I had waited for you. John had have killed HN by then!" Roma said.

"But, still. There's something wrong with him!" Meera said, quickly jumped up on her car and drove after the police.

Roma went to the hospital to see HN. He had few injuries but was fine. He was resting, when Roma came.

"Is John okay?" he asked.

"I suppose," Roma answered.

"Suppose?" HN said in a confused way.

"I mean, I exactly don't know. He's with the police right now," Roma said.

In the police station, things were not going in favor of John.

"I'm sorry?! I'm, mean, sir, you're an official detective and you don't know rules of law," the officer said.

"I must say, Mr. Duncan, you don't know the plan Psycho is working on. He's up to something very big," John said

"I'm leaving you off with a warning," Mr. Duncan, the officer said.

Meera and John came out of the office.

"Why? Why did you attack HN?" Meera asked furiously.

"Because he's Psycho! You know that, don't you!" John said.

"But he denied it!"

"He could be lying!"

"Look, Psycho can control people, ok. Maybe he could've brought HN under control and forced him to act as Psycho."

"What if it's not true?"

"There's a 99% possibility. After knowing that you somehow doubt HN, Psycho could've used him!"

John couldn't counter that because Meera was right. Still, he had a full doubt HN was Psycho. John's phone rang the very moment and he picked up.

"Ha, ha, ha!" laughter was heard.

"Psycho? Right!" John quickly guessed.

"Yes! Good guessing!" Psycho answered.

"What now?"

"I like playing games with you. Do you remember when HN told you that you couldn't get Psycho until and unless he doesn't want you to?"

"Yes, I do!"

"Good! Right now I'm not in a mood for you to get me. So, you won't."

"I know it's you HN!"

"HN? What a lovely pal he is! Don't make me feel like he's a danger to my work. Look you should've understood that HN is an innocent boy. I just set him up to mislead you," Psycho hung up.

John looked at Meera and said, "I think you're right. Psycho did set up HN. I should apologize to him and Roma for my behavior."

Both of them visited the hospital where the nurse said they had already gone home. Meera asked Roma where she was. Then they went to HN's house. Reaching there, they explained everything.

"I apologize, HN," John said.

"You don't have to. It's okay. We understand Psycho was misleading you," HN said.

"Can't believe Psycho could do such a thing," Roma said.

"Two things are clear to me now. If Psycho controls someone and then releases him, the person doesn't remember anything and he was misleading me for some important reason," John said.

"You're right. But what could the reason be?" Meera said.

"That's what I'm musing about right now," John answered.

"Is it okay, if I say something?" HN asked.

"Yeah, go ahead, speak up," John replied.

"Maybe Psycho was misleading me to mislead you," HN said

The other three in the room looked at him with the most confused face.

"I mean maybe he was misleading you so that when he revealed to you something, your actions will be focused to resolve that thing," HN explained.

"Maybe or maybe not," John said.

"It's true! How many times have we crammed our ideas to the fact that Psycho uses common sense more than intelligence?" Roma said.

"Roma's right." Meera said.

"Looks like I find myself stranded in the middle of nowhere," John said.

A spotless sky of May welcomed the morning of the Americans. It was the first day of May. The sky was bright blue with the most pulchritudinous sun shining brighter than ever. The day began most appealingly and pleasantly. But nothing is too long lasted. By mid-day, news came that twenty business officials had capitulated to death, around the world. These business officials belonged to twenty different countries. These were the USA, UK, France, Italy, Japan, South Korea, Russia, India, Pakistan, Brazil, Spain, Germany, Australia, New Zealand, Ukraine, Turkey, Iran, Saudi Arabia, China, and Canada.

John was not at all angry but sad he was. Well, he knew Psycho would do something on May Day so he expected bad news.

"What more can we expect from a serial criminal, a killer?" John said regretfully.

"I know, so what's our plan?" Meera asked.

"Seriously, I don't know. I'm stuck in a desert. I can't have mirage even!" John replied.

"John, who can't give up that easily."

"I'm not! It's just I don't have any idea. I haven't faced that kind of criminal in my life ever before. I'm usually done with criminals in a matter of weeks or sometimes a month, but months is way too much."

Meera clasped John and said.

"I know you can, I know you will."

Roma came in the very moment and smiled at the two lovers. Then she was reminded of her lover.

"Thinking about me?" HN came from behind.

"Pff! No. I was looking at Meera and John," Roma said.

"Okay. Then why am I here?" I thought somebody was thinking about me," HN said.

"Huh, Ha! No one!" Roma said and went out. HN followed.

The day was of bliss and blues, John still regretting the death of the business officials. In the evening, Meera invited John, Roma, and HN over dinner. Tee also accompanied her sister. Meera was a great cook. She cooked for the four most delicious cuisines. John remarked that he was lucky to be getting married to Meera.

"HN, why don't you have some more?" Meera insisted.

"No, no, thanks. I have had enough. I don't eat much," HN said.

"That's why you look so weak!" John teased.

Everyone laughed.

"No, not the case at all," HN said.

"Come on! Open up a little bit. Say something about yourself!" Meera said.

"Like what?" HN said.

"How about we know who your parents were?"

On this thing, HN's smile faded and he went in a flash-back of when he had heard the news of the death of his parents and his journey thereafter.

"Why don't we all talk about our parents. That'd motivate him to talk about his," John said and everyone agreed.

"My mom is a high school biology teacher. My dad is a football coach," Meera said, "We used to have so much fun back in California before we moved here."

Everybody started discussing their parents, what they did, how much they loved them, and everything else. HN couldn't handle it anymore and burst out, "Not everyone enjoys living with their parents!"

He went crying, leaving the group confused and perplexed. Roma got up and came to him. He was crying silently under the moonlight.
"What happened?" She asked.
"I'm not lucky as you guys. You at least get to talk to your parents, Roma. But mine is just too far from me, too far that I can't even see them. I don't even remember how they used to take care of me. My parents are dead!" HN said.
"Don't cry. We are sorry about this come we'll talk about something else." Roma said.
"No. thanks. I'll leave now," HN said.
"Why?"
"I just don't love talking much with people. I'm not a social guy."
"Yes, you are, you idiot!" Roma patted HN's back.
"No, I'm not. Now let me go. I've to check some assignments," HN went fading into the dark, barely lit road. Roma stood looking at the evanescing figure. John also came out and said, "Everything ok?"
"Yeah! I suppose he's just a little tired," Roma said.
"We should've considered asking him why didn't he talk about his parents," John added.
Roma went in. She seemed upset.

So, the unwanted day died down and a new day came up with hopes and expectations, for not only the world but John too. John began the morning by looking at all the case files against Psycho, in the hope to come up with a clue.
"Phew! This guy's so tough!" John said to himself.
Looking at reports, turning the pages, John continued his indefatigable search for clues. Meera came in and saw John

occupied in work. She smiled and addressed, "Well, look at you. You're so busy, aren't you?'

"Yeah, dead busy. You don't want to know," John replied.

"Any clue?"

"No, but shouldn't lose hope."

"Keep it up!" Meera gave a caress on John's back.

Roma also arrived but with a friend. And it was not HN!

"Guy, I want you to meet a nice friend of mine, a childhood friend," Roma said.

The two looked at the friend of Roma, a boy he was. Not much tall, of some average height. But good. He had a faux hawk haircut, hair dyed in red. His eyes had a deep blue color and he looked very attractive.

"Wow, who's he?" Meera asked.

"My childhood best friend, Enrique Owen," Roma said.

"And Enrique, this is Meera and this is John."

"Hi, nice to meet you," Enrique held his hands to Meera for a shake.

"Whoa! Whoa! Back off young man. Don't mean to scare you. But this angel beauty, right here. She's taken," John said jealously.

"I'm sorry. It was just a friendly shake," Enrique said.

"Mr. John Waven, do you mind taking your arm off me!" Meera said in a controlling manner.

John lifted his arm off Meera. Roma giggled a little and said, "Enrique's parents just moved to D.C today. He and I used to be friends, back when I live in San Francisco. But when my mom and dad brought me here. I missed him a lot!"

"Ok, so a reunion of friends," Meera said.

"Mmm! So now you can recollect memories and share, right?" John said.

"Yeah!" Enrique said.

"Good, do that and move out," John pushed the two young friends out of the room.

Meera looked at him in a questioning manner.

"He could be Psycho! Who knows!" John said.

"Why everyone could be Psycho?" Meera asked.

"Because she's innocent, You're innocent and Psycho targets, innocent people. Duh!" John replied.

"You're jealous. I get it," Meera said.

"No, I'm not!" said John, and Meera continued teasing him.

Roma went out with Enrique and the first thought which came to her mind was to make him meet HN.

"I'll take you to meet someone special." She said.

"Whom?" Enrique asked.

The two were walking towards the college gate when HN saw Roma and started approaching her.

"Who's this guy with Roma?" He thought.

"Hey, HN! Hi!" Roma waved at him.

"Hi, Roma. I see you got a new friend," HN said.

"Not new. He's my childhood friend, Enrique," Roma said.

"Oh, I see," HN said.

"Enrique, this is HN. My friend and my teacher too," Roma said.

The boys got introduced to each other and some ceremonial things took place, hugs, and handshakes.

"So, you coming to college?" HN asked.

"No, I might skip it for today. I'm thinking of taking Enrique around a little. You know spend some time with him," Roma said.

HN's smile faded and a furious look took over.

"NO!" he said.

Roma looked at him in a questioning manner.

"I mean, why today? You could take him tomorrow," HN said.

"It's because it's better today than tomorrow. And I've missed him a lot, so I can't wait," Roma said.

"OK, I won't interfere," HN left the two with a sad face.

Enrique turned to Roma,

"I think your friend doesn't want us to spend time."

"No, he's fine. I suppose." Roma said in a fancy way although inside she kind of thought that Enrique was right.

Back to the two investigators, John and Meera.

Meera came to John holding a file in black cover.

"This file here says that nearly 100,000 pitiful criminals have died all around the world. And some 1300, high-profiled criminals have also died," Meera said.

"That's how many people have died because of Psycho's work?" John said surprised.

"Yes! This is bad," Meera said.

"But I promise it Meera that this won't last long. Psycho will surrender," John said.

The two continued with research while Roma was having fun with Enrique. They were in a local park, sitting on a bench and eating ice cream. HN was in the park too, looking at the two.

"You lied!" he said to himself, "You said you were my friend, that you'd enjoy with me and no one else!"

He got up and walked towards the two.

"Hey, HN. What a coincidence?" Roma said.

"Hey, hi, I was just about to have a walk by the beach, thought you'd like to join?" HN said.

"Why not! Enrique can come too, right?" Roma said.

"Huh! I just remembered that I had some important work to complete. So, anytime later. Bye!" HN dared towards the road and went away.

"Wow, your friend's so odd!" Enrique said.

HN arrived at his house, smashing the door came in.

"You're going to pay for acting like this Roma!" He shouted.

11

THE ESTRANGEMENT

A black limo entered the propinquity of the White House. A young gentleman, around his twenties dressed in a black coat, white shirt, black trousers, and black tie, He was wearing glasses too. Come out of it.

The officials came to him, surrounded by guards.

"Who are you?" an official asked.

"Your doom," the young man answered.

The officials laughed and said, "It's not a scene of a movie, young man. Its reality!"

The guards pointed the gun at him.

The young man smiled and said, "I'm aware of its reality!"

The guards suddenly turned the guns on the officials and started firing on them.

"Hahahaha!" the young man laughed out loud. "Happy Death Day!"

The man left the scene while the police arrived thereafter he was gone.

Not a single person on the spot was left alive. The stream of blood lay on the feet of the White House.

The news soon came knocking at John's door.

"What?!" John raised in horror.

"Yes, that's right, sir," the caller said.

"You're saying that they were shot by the guards themselves?" John said.

"Yes! Unusual, I know. But it's the truth," the caller answered.

"I'm coming!"

John quickly drove off to White House. The whole area was surrounded by the army, officials, and the FBI investigation team. Media too had a share of the land.

"I haven't had any call from Psycho. Is it that he didn't do anything?" John thought.

Roma was in a café with Enrique when she had a call from HN.

"Yes, HN. Anything important?" she said.

"Important? Don't you know?" HN said.

"What?"

"A shocking scene took place at the White House, it's all over the news now!"

She lifted her bag and ran to catch a cab.

Enrique was left in the café.

A guy approached him and whispered from behind, "She's dead!"

Enrique turned around but he was gone. He got worried and followed Roma to the white House. On the gate, that same young man was standing.

"Enrique, I've been waiting for you," he said.

"Who are you?" Enrique asked.

The man was wearing a mask and he removed it.

"HN?" Enrique was surprised.

"Why, yes! It is me!" HN smiled.

"What do you think you're doing here?" Enrique asked.

"And same for you," HN said.

"I'm here for Roma!" Enrique replied.

"Good! Come here, I'll take you to her."

John was talking to some officials when his phone rang.

"John, sorry to disturb you, but this is very important!" the caller said.

"Is it you HN?" John asked.

"Yes! Look, I'm in my house right now and I think there is someone, unusually dressed standing outside," HN said.

"Do you think it's Psycho?" John questioned.

"Maybe. Just tell me what shall I do."

"Don't come out. Wait there. I'll be there soon!" John hung up.

"HN Maaki, I know you're Psycho!" John said.

He quickly reached HN's house. There was a guy, indeed but John struck his head and made him unconscious.

He rang the bell and hid.

HN opened the door and saw the guy lying down.

"I know you're here John," he said out loud.

"Well, how did you? Psycho!" John said.

"I'm HN, not Psycho. What's wrong with you?"

"I doubted you even after the kidnapping of Roma. One thing today cleared it. When I asked Roma how did she know about the shooting she said she told him that it was all over the news. But the media didn't broadcast the news because I told them not to !" John said.

"Well, well," HN came down the staircases, clapping his hands. "So much for your intelligence, John. You still cannot beat me."

John assailed HN and punched him. And hand combat started.

Back to the White House, where Roma's eyes caught sight of Enrique.

"Enrique? What's he doing here?" she thought.

She ran to him and asked him what he was doing here.

Getting back to the fight, John and HN, both had a run of energy now.

"Look, you might have come here to show me a light of your dumb intelligence but if you had been that much intelligent that you'd have wondered why did I bring you here!" HN smiled.

John paused for a moment and went into flashback. He remembered watching Enrique near the park of the White House.

"What did you do to Enrique?!" John said.

HN laughed hard and said," How foolish of you. In a rush to catch of me you didn't notice Enrique."

Enrique had forcibly taken Roma with him to a ruined building. He then had tied her up there and left her alone. He came to HN and said that he had done his work.

"What work?" John said.

"Dear, John, it's too late for you now!" HN went in, leaving the confused John alone with Enrique.

He turned to Enrique and said, "What happened?" Enrique fell unconscious. John ran to him and held him in his arms. John called the ambulance and he called Meera.

The ambulance took Enrique, while John and Meera followed up.

"Are you crazy?" Meera said after listening to John's story.

"No, I'm not. Except for that one way of the other I was bound to fall into a trap," John replied.

"But I thought we were done with then 'HN being Psycho' thing," Meera said.

"Yeah, I know. But c'mon, see the big picture. He was fooling us."

"Ok, but where's Roma?"

"Reporting! Obviously."

"What if not! Let's go and check," Meera said, "On second thought I think I should go. You stay with Enrique.

John held Meera's hands and said, "Take care!"

Meera drove to the White House in giffy. There she got to know that Roma was not there. She called John and told him that Roma wasn't there.

"No! But why'd HN kidnap her?" John asked.

"Why should I know, but it seems paradoxical," Meera said.

Roma was alone, tied up in a dump, dark ruined building with not a single soul around.

"Help! Someone help!" she called out.

A sound of clap answered her call.

"Who is it?" Roma asked.

A dark figure came into light. It was Psycho, dressed in the same gentleman suit but was wearing a mask.

"Are you Psycho?" she asked.

"Yes, yes I am. So how have you been lately?" Psycho asked.

"I'm fine! Thanks for asking!" Roma said.

"I've been observing you lately and let me be honest with you. I like you, Roma!" Psycho said.

Roma looked surprisingly at Psycho,

"Are-Are you crazy!" she said.

"Yes! Yes, I am! Just because you say doesn't mean I am. This is what everyone said but I'm not crazy. I am normal like you. I've right to live, I'm a human too!"

"No, you're not! Someone who kills people brutally isn't worth being called a human!'

"What about a boy whose parents died and the culprits weren't ever caught again! And the boy was taken to asylum without any reason."

Roma went silent. She had nothing to say.

"What's the matter? Why you are quiet now? Have nothing to say," Psycho said.

"That boy deserves justice. But not at the cost of other human beings!" Roma said.

"That's what I like about Roma," Psycho said.

Psycho untied Roma and held her hands and took her outside.

"I don't know how to explain this world is a dirty place. It's so difficult to breathe and to tell how you feel. All the questions in my mind and so much to decide. The only thing comforting when you're by my side."

Psycho kissed Roma's forehead and a drop of tear from his eyes fell on Roma's cheeks. There was a moment of silence. Roma felt as if it was HN standing close to her.

Meera and John were worried about Roma. They didn't have any clue about where she was. Enrique hadn't become conscious yet.

"What do we do now?" Meera said.

"I don't know! Ok!" John said furiously.

"Why are you so angry?"

"I'm angry over HN. If he does something to Roma, I'll kill him for sure. Roma's like my sister."

"Ok, ok! Easy, let's check the CCTV around the White House."

"It'd have worked if it wasn't for Psycho. He'd have meddled with the CCTV of the area."

"You're right: But still let's give it a try."

Both went to see. But as John expected, the cameras weren't working. Disappointed, Meera and John headed back to the hospital. It was evening by now. The sun had almost gone into hiding.

John still was working on tracing Roma and Meera had gone to stay with Tee until Roma came.

Roma was with Psycho near a lake.
"Why do you?" Roma said.
"Do what?" Psycho said.
"Like me!"
"Because you're special Roma. You're unique."
"How do you know so much about me?"
Psycho put his finger on Roma's lips and said, "Quiet listen to the sound."
There was a sound of joy. People moving in joy, children playing and music. The city seemed to be lighted up for something special.
"This is sound of the satisfaction of the people who have been given justice," Psycho said.
"Everything seems so different," Roma got up.
"Is there anyone special to you like you're to me?" Psycho asked. He thought and expected, Roma to say Enrique was special to him. But her answer startled him.
"Yes, there is. He's someone unique. The day I met him I expected that he'd be normal like everyone else but he proved me wrong. He's the only one I trust the most!" Roma said.
"And who's he?" Psycho asked.
"A person special to me, HN," Roma looked up and closed her eyes.
Psycho stood motionless.
"And I think I love him," Roma said.
Psycho held her hands and said, "Then you deserve to go back to him."
He took her to his limo and drove her to HN's house.
"I might love you, but I think his love for you might be more powerful," Psycho said and drove away.
Roma ran to HN's house and rang the bell. HN opened the door and as soon as he saw her, he hugged her.

"I was worried sick about you, Roma. I called you a dozen times but you didn't answer. Is everything okay?" he asked.

"Yes, HN. I'm fine. I need to talk to you," Roma closed the door and seated herself comfortably.

"HN, since Enrique came, you've been acting oddly. Is it because you were jealous?" Roma asked.

"I…. I don't know," HN answered.

"Please, don't confuse me."

"Ok, fine. Maybe I was jealous, after all."

"HN, no one can replace you in my life, ever!" Roma got up and gave a very friendly hug to HN.

"Roma, thanks," HN said and a drop of tear came running down his cheeks.

"And one more important thing. I love you, HN."

HN became silent. He didn't reply for some time and then he broke the silence, "I love you, too!"

Well, well, that's enough for romantic scenes here. It's a serious book, come on people!

Roma got up and said, "I should call John. He'd be worried about me."

Roma called John and he and Meera both quickly arrived at HN's place with Enrique.

John hugged Roma and then did Meera. Enrique also has a friendly hug.

John looked at HN and he stared back.

"What game are you playing now?" John thought.

Meera looked at HN. He had turned his eyes on Roma and was smiling at her. Then she looked at John. He was still looking at HN.

"Would it kill you a little to look at me and smile?" She said.

"What?" John said confused.

"Yes, Mr. soon-to-be-husband!"

"Meera, are you okay?" John put his hand on Meera's forehead. "You're never interested in flirting with me."

"Now, I am. Got it!"

"No, I don't. where is my 'angry Meera.?"

"I'm joking!" Meera laughed and John sighed.

The group sat for a while to ask Roma about what exactly happened.

"When I called for help, Psycho came in clapping. Then he took me out of the lake. I don't know what was he up to," she said.

John was confused by the story. It appeared as if there were some missing links. There was something Roma hadn't expressed.

HN too felt the same way.

"Why didn't Roma say the thing Psycho told her? Why's she hiding it?" he thought.

"What happened between Roma and Psycho that she is hiding?" John thought.

"If I tell anyone the truth that Psycho likes me it'll be considered as his weakness. And who knows if I go ahead and say something like this it might break HN's heart," Roma mused.

Meera was looking at the faces of the three musing minds. She knew something was going on in their heads.

"Ok, John and I shall leave now. We've got work to do." She said and holding John's hand brought him out.

"Why were you staring at Roma? Is everything okay?" Meera said.

"I feel the story she narrated was incomplete. There were some missing links," John replied.

"Whatever you think. Let's go."

Both went to the office to do the work.

Roma left with Enrique to her home. HN stood at the balcony thinking.

"What was I thinking? I was about to hurt Roma. Thank God I didn't!" he thought.

The next morning, John visited Roma to ask some questions.

"I swear I'm not hiding anything, John," Roma said.

"Well, you're. The story seems confusing that simply means there were missing links. I want to know," John said.

"Fine. Psycho said he likes me!" Roma said.

"What! Did he?"

"Yes, he did."

John was shocked like Roma was. This thing confirmed HN was Psycho.

"I knew it!" John got up.

"Knew what?" Roma asked.

"Nothing, anyways, I'll go!" John rushed to meet Meera.

On the way, he met HN.

"Hello, how are you doing?" HN asked.

"I'm fine. Roma told me everything. And now there's no turning back. You're Psycho," John said.

"I don't care, right now. You know what you can't still prove anything even if you put on that confidence."

"Because I am confident!"

12

RECTITUDE OF INQUIRY : VISION OF THE WORLD

John told everything to Meera and she was shocked too. She didn't expect it.

"That means you're right! HN is Psycho after all."

"And he's using Roma's innocent love for him for his selfish purposes," John said.

"Or maybe not. Both times when Psycho, say HN, kidnapped Roma he didn't hurt her or anything. Maybe he loves her too. After all, Roma is a great person," Meera said.

John looked at her curiously. He didn't get why'd Meera say such a thing in the first place, anyways.

"Are you nuts?" John said.

"No!" Meera said.

John didn't accept the thought that HN loved Roma. A psycho who kills people can never have a heart that loves.

"Listen, if you think with your heart for a moment you can see HN's love for Roma," Meera tried to make John understand.

"Even if I do, I still think HN as a killer and not a lover!" John said out in a loud voice.

"John calm down! Fine, HN doesn't love Roma," Meera said and went to her room.

John followed her and quietly came into the room. Slowly and steadily he went towards Meera and hugged her from behind.

“I’m sorry! Did I make my Meera angry?” he said.

Meera smiled and said, “It’s okay. We cannot share the same point of view.”

The two sat for a discussion once again.

Meanwhile, Roma and HN were having some friend time in a coffee shop.

“Roma for some reason, John still thinks I’m Psycho,” HN said.

“Why’d he? I think you got it wrong. Anyways why are we discussing Psycho,” Roma said.

The two were talking when a nearby table broke into a fight.

“You break my glass and now you hit me on my face!” one of the guys said.

The other guy, his opponent, pushed him hard while his group handled him. The guys started punching and hitting each other.

HN rushed to them and in loud voice said, “Stop!”

The guys turned towards him.

“What’s wrong,” he asked.

One of the guys answered, “Marco broke my glass and when I asked, he hit me on my face.”

Marco interrupted and said,” No! He didn’t ask anything instead he started calling me bad words.

“Oh no I didn't !” The guy said.

“Look, whatever the case may be did you hit him?” HN asked Marco.

“Yes I did but..” Marco replied but was interrupted.

"No ifs and buts. I just asked if you hit him, that's it. Apologize! And for you whatever your name is why did he hit you in the first place," HN said.

The guy said, "It's Jonas. By the way who are you to decide anything! He hit me because I accidentally broke his glass. Am I wrong?"

"No, he didn't break anything he used bad language!" Marco said.

"I asked you to apologize and not escalate this situation anymore," HN said to Marco.

Roma didn't have a good feeling about the situation. Marco wasn't an easy person, so he punched HN right on his chest, hard fist.

"HN!" Roma quickly held him.

"It's okay I'm fine Roma," HN assured her.

Now HN couldn't bear it anymore, so, he held Marco by his collar. Marco's friends rose to his defense and gathered around. A chaotic atmosphere builds up. Even other people from the shop came to HN's defense and a fight broke between the groups.

Roma quickly called the police and John. The police reached there quickly and stopped the fight. HN came towards Roma. He had some scratches and a wound around his arm and face. Marco was lying on the floor. The police secured him and called in the medics.

"He's dead, sir," said one of the officers.

John arrived there the very moment.

"Is everything okay Roma?" He asked.

"I suppose except for that pitiful guy," Roma said pointing towards Marco.

"What happened to him?" John asked.

"He died during the chaos. Unusual right?" Roma answered.

John at once understood what could have happened.
He knew that HN could have done something wrong with that guy.
It was all very simple. HN created the fight so many people were pushing and hitting each other. This would have created an atmosphere of anarchy, giving HN a full chance of using his power to kill the guy. This way no one could see him using his power and the guy's death would be credited to the stampede during the fight.
Looking at John's out of box expression, Roma asked, "Everything okay?"
"Yeah, *Todo Bien*?" John answered.
With a little Spanish, John went to the police.
HN looked at him and knew that John had guessed what could have happened. He went with Roma without any worry.
'Small battles are no edition to big ones,' HN smiled to himself.

John went back to Meera after discussing the situation with the police. He explained everything to Meera
"So exactly why did he kill him?" Meera asked.
"Because Marco hit him on his chest and refused to do what he said. C'mon he is the Psycho" John replied taking in a sip of tea.
"What is the chance that it can make Roma believe that HN is psycho?"
John got off his chair and walked towards the window, "I have got a brilliant idea!"
HN sat beside Roma watching the surroundings of her garden.
"So, Roma, anything special?" HN asked.

"Nothing much. I am still confused, how did the guy die?" Roma asked.

"It is ok, don't pressure yourself that much. Take it easy."

Roma put her head on HN's shoulder and thought, "How can I ever say to HN that I doubt that he killed the guy. Is John's right, HN is Psycho? After all both the guys like me."

HN was thinking, what if his truth got revealed, how would Roma react.

Both thinking almost the same thing held their hands tight and closed their eyes.

Suddenly Roma got up and said. "HN I can't be friends with you anymore."

She left leaving HN confused.

"Roma! What is wrong?!" he called to her but she didn't respond.

He ran after her and stopped her.

"Answer me!" he said.

"Because I think you are Psycho!" she said.

HN looked at her with nothing to say. He, heartbroken, left for his house.

After reaching, he laid down himself on the bed and started crying and screaming.

"John Waven! You are so in trouble!" he shouted.

John was in his room all alone thinking and watching the news.

'Now moving to the next report people are disappearing from different countries and are being found dead near water bodies or some barren land.' The reporter said.

John looked at this news with amazement.

"What ?" he said.

"Although this could be related to Psycho, forensics found that the dead bodies have signs that some kind of weapon had been used," the report said. "Government official said that they were looking into this matter and will soon find the culprit behind it. Is it a birth of a new Psycho?"

John held his head in despair. What the heck was this?

He quickly called Meera and told her to come over.

Meera did come, although she was tired.

"What now?" she asked.

"Did you hear the news?" John asked.

"No, I was tired!" she replied furiously.

John calmly explained everything and left her wide-eyed.

"If it isn't Psycho, who is it?" she asked.

"That is what I am thinking. We have barely even caught this Psycho, we can't handle yet another!" John said.

"Oh, God what is happening to this world."

The next morning, HN arrived to meet John who had a very uncomfortable night twisting and thinking about the situation going around the world. His doorbell rang loudly and he came down to open it.

"Who's it?" John asked half sleepy.

"Hironaga Maaki, a.k.a HN."

John opened the door in surprise.

"Woah! Oh! Good morning Psycho." He said.

"I am not very happy today Mr. Waven. Don't make me angry. Do you know what you have done?" HN said.

"What? Exposed you or something else!"

"You took everything I had! It is because you had to say to Roma that I was Psycho and now she doesn't want to be with me, because she thinks I am Psycho!" HN held John by his collar.

"Really ?! Christmas for me!"

"It isn't funny." HN started crying and put his head leaning on John's chest.

John couldn't understand what was happening. HN, being Psycho, should have already played a game to take revenge from John or Roma but he didn't.

"Why aren't you doing anything? You have got the power to control people so why don't you control Roma and make her friend again," John said.

HN gave a psychotic laugh and said, "will I ever get what Roma could give me when she is herself?"

"No, but, you know," John said.

"She is the only person I will never control. I like her when she is herself."

John went quiet. HN came close to him and whispered, "If I wanted I would have killed you a long ago. The only reason you are still alive is my Roma!"

John pushed him back and said. "You deserve it. What else can I say?"

John turned around to go.

"Wait, stop!" HN cried.

John saw HN down on his knees.

"I am begging you! Please bring me my Roma back," he said.

"Are you crazy? What are you doing?" John said.

"I love her and if she leaves me I will have no person in my life who will ever promise me to be with me. She is the only reason I am living!" HN said crying badly.

John understood that Meera was right, HN did like Roma very much. But he didn't want to break Roma's heart, so he refused to help HN. He knew once he is caught, Roma will be the one who will be the most hurt.

HN got up and said, "You're gonna pay for it, John."

He went away leaving John worried. He knew he was gonna hurt Meera. But how?

Late night, around half-past ten, John got a call from an unknown number. Once he picked up a panting and worried voice answered.

"I need your help!" the Caller said.

"Who are you?" John asked.

"I am Dr. Ben. I am in a club and I think Psycho is here too. I am the one who was treating him. He is after me. He already killed some of my friends."

"Where are you?" John asked.

"I am in the Eden Lounge DC club," he replied.

"You got it! I will be there in about fifteen minutes. Try to be safe," John hung up and quickly drove to the FBI office, his house being not very far from there. There he called Meera and Roma and told them to come to the club.

John brought himself a gun and drove right away to the club, his car breaking the speed limits. However, on the way, there had been an accident that had taken place and the road was blocked, so John got delayed. When he reached, Meera and Roma were already there.

"What timing!" Meera said.

"I got caught up in a jam. Let us go," John said.

Soon the three entered with their guns in their hands stealthily. They first tried to find this guy, Dr. Ben. But found none, instead, they stumbled upon four dead found lying at the same place with gunshots at their heads.

"We are late! I think we still have a chance of finding Psycho. Let's go," John said.

Disappointed a bit, the three looked around expecting to come across Psycho. Unusual for them, everyone there in the club was dressed in a hooded jacket with a cap and face mask.

But they still kept searching. Each one of them felt that someone was following them. Roma and John ended up catching the same person, thinking he was Psycho.

Meera was still searching when someone ran his hands through her mouth and held her hand behind her back. Slowly he pulled her out of the club and tied her hands, put a cloth around her mouth and eyes. Then he pushed her into a car and started the journey.

"Aw, man! He is some innocent guy" Roma said.

"We are fools. I hope Meera found him…" John paused.

His heart throbbed out of fear and he got paralyzed.

"What is wrong John?" Roma asked.

Soon his phone rang and he had to pick it up as he knew it was Psycho and he had Meera.

"Hahaha! I am amused by your eagerness to catch me, John," Psycho said.

"Where is Meera?" John asked.

"Well, lying on a cold stone floor. Expecting you."

"Don't you hurt her, leave her alone."

"Should have done this very much long ago but now is much more satisfying!"

Suddenly John heard gunshots, three in a row. He went silent.

"Meera!" He cried.

"Hahahahah! She is alright. I didn't kill her but I will if you don't do what I will say. Got it!" Psycho said. "And don't involve Roma or else I don't know, maybe her dead body will reach you soon."

"Ok fine," John said.

"Good, I will call you after you have left the club." Psycho hung up.

Roma had stood there watching all of this, getting more and more confused. When she asked what had happened, John put the answer in a nutshell and went away home.

"How can I save Meera..." John said.

13

THE BIRTH OF MILLINIEUM

Oshika, Nagano, Japan:

Oshika, the mountainous beauty, the home of Psycho. He was born there in one of the richest families of the village, the Maaki family. The boy was welcomed by the whole village. He was named Hironaga, shortly called HN. By birth, he was a quiet person and by age, he became a shy one too. However, not much shy in front of the villagers with whom he worked and played. After school, every day he would go out to play in the forest with some other boys from the village. Until the day when he was told that he and his family were shifting to America, HN was the happiest person. And all of a sudden he lost all his happiness to the cruel world.

NPA, Japan, Tokyo, Chiyoda:

Officer Hiromi and some other officials sat in a meeting.

"It is our final decision. We will do it." She said.

The other officers nodded their heads to agree and the meeting was over. Hiromi called in to prepare a plane to Washington DC.

John was already occupied with Psycho's given task. He had to go to the FBI office and bring all information about Psycho to him so that he can destroy it.

John packed all the required stuff and went to meet Psycho.

He was waiting near an old building, whose doors were rusted.

"I hope you got me what I needed, " Psycho said.

"Yes, I did. Show me Meera!" John said.

Psycho pressed a button near one of the doors of the building.

A guy came out along with Meera and left.

"Files, Meera" Psycho said.

John handed over the files and got his Meera.

"Now for the surprise HN," John said and all of a sudden a whole bunch of cops surrounded Psycho. There was a team of doctors too. Roma also came in soon.

"No! Leave me!" HN said while his hands were being tied.

"How is that for a Christmas gift! Psycho a.k.a HN" John said.

Roma looked at HN, heartbroken.

"Roma, please listen to me," HN said.

"I don't want to hear anything, I hate you," Roma said.

"Please Roma" HN cried.

He started screaming and hit an officer. He ran right to Roma when a doctor hit him with an injection to make him unconscious. He felt right in front of Roma.

Roma went away crying while Meera followed.

"I will take him," Hiromi came.

"He is all yours until the decision comes," John said.

"Thanks. I shall leave." Hiromi bid him goodbye and left with HN.

When HN opened his eyes he found himself far away from Roma, in an asylum in Japan.

"You will have to see how it feels to lose someone you love the most Roma," HN said.

Six months later:

Roma sat in her room near a window trying to remember HN's comforting smile, which he usually gave her when she was sad or depressed. The very moment Tee came in.

"You ok sister? Missing HN, right?" she asked.

"Yeah, can't get him out of my head. It's been like six months already." Roma said.

"It is ok. You can never forget someone you loved."

"Right, anyway, I will go to meet John and Meera. See ya!"

Roma set out to meet John and Meera who were having lunch.

"May I?" She asked.

"Oh yeah, of course," Meera said.

"What is up?" John asked.

"Nothing much. Mom wants me to come back to California." Roma answered.

"Really, great. At least you can get your head off HN," John said.

"Yeah, whatever. What's the news from Japan?" Roma asked.

"Ain't got anything yet. Still, let's see."

When John said it, Meera turned on the TV. The reporter was reporting from a site of the blast.

'A blast in a mall has taken place in California. Luckily there was no one inside except for the owner of the mall who was tied inside.' The Reporter said.

"What?! What kind of murder style is this?" John said.

A man loyal to HN shifted all the information and plans to a different base, so the police didn't find any kind of proof. He traveled to HN's home in Japan and kept everything hidden there, safe from everyone.

He wrote an email and sent it to all the people around the world.

'*To all those people who support Psycho, I have an important message for all of you. To keep Psycho's idea alive, you may like to join a worldwide group against political tyranny, The MILLINIEUM!'*

The email knocked doors for John too.

"Millinieum?!" he jumped off his chair.

John showed the email to both the gals next to him. His phone rang in a moment and it was Hiromi.

"HN escaped! He is probably on his way to America." Hiromi warned.

John was dumbfounded.

"No, this can't happen." He thought.

"Roma go home. Check-in on your sister. HN has escaped and he is definitely on his way to America." John said.

Without uttering anything but her face clearly showing her worry, Roma rushed off to her house. But she was late. HN was already there, waiting at the door.

"Konichiwa! Roma." He said.

"You didn't do anything to my sister?!!" she said worryingly.

"No, I didn't but she will," he answered.

Roma didn't like the answer, so she quickly went in where Tee had already lifted a gun.

"No, Tee, please stop!" she said.

But Tee didn't listen and shot herself right on spot.

"Tee!!!' Roma yelled out in terror.

"Why did you do this, HN?!" she said crying.

"It's my revenge on you. You lied. You never were my friend." HN said.

Suddenly a bunch of policemen called from outside that the house had been surrounded. John came into the house and assailed towards HN.

"You've done enough! HN!" he said while holding him off.

HN started resisting but couldn't free himself. Suddenly there was a gunshot. Blood came out of HN's arm and yet another shot on his head and he died on spot.

"Roma, what have you done?" John was shocked.

"I had no choice. He killed Tee, he was struggling and I couldn't see his pain!" she said.

Doctors and other officials were called. HN's body was taken away and Tee's body too.

Nothing related to Psycho's death was given out to the public. The case was kept closed and secret. Soon with time Psycho's name faded.

But not from Roma's mind. She went back to California to her family, broken-hearted. She had lost the two most important persons at the same time.

John was packing his stuff. His mind was occupied not only with HN's death but this new group Millinieum

Meera came in and put her hand on John's shoulder.

"So, what is next?" she said.

"Oh. IDK. Anyways, I'll have to leave," He said.

"IDK?! You are a detective! Come on."

"Oh, hey! Will you marry me?"

Meera smiled and hugged him. "Now that's it."

Someone ringed the bell and delivered a letter.

John took it and opened it.

"*You may have killed Psycho, but you didn't kill his ideology. He will live as long as people oppose tyranny. Long live Psycho!!! Head of Millinieum.*"

John, after reading it, didn't know what to say Meera. Meera just grabbed the letter.

She read it but before giving him a reaction she found something on the back.

"***Do you think John, you caught me because you were intelligent. I told you, you won't ever catch me until and unless I wish you to catch me. Whatever happened was your surprise for me. The Millinieum is my surprise for you. Over 183 bases in different countries all around the world and the real base, you will never find it. Looks like I win at the end!!***"

www.ingramcontent.com/pod-product-compliance
Ingram Content Group UK Ltd.
Pitfield, Milton Keynes, MK11 3LW, UK
UKHW042017190726
13854UKWH00005B/2326